T0208983

Stories of God

Stories of God

Rainer Maria
Rilke

A New Translation by
MICHAEL H. KOHN

Shambhala
BOSTON & LONDON
2003

SHAMBHALA PUBLICATIONS, INC.
Horticultural Hall
300 Massachusetts Avenue
Boston, Massachusetts 02115
www.shambhala.com

Printed in the United States of America

♾ This edition is printed on acid-free paper that meets the American National Standards Institute Z39.48 Standard.
♻ Shambhala Publications makes every effort to print on recycled paper. For more information please visit www.shambhala.com.
Distributed in the United States by Penguin Random House LLC and in Canada by Random House of Canada Ltd

Library of Congress Cataloging-in-Publication Data
Rilke, Rainer Maria, 1875–1926.
[Geschichten vom lieben Gott. English]
Stories of God/Rainer Maria Rilke; a new translation by Michael H. Kohn.
p. cm.
ISBN 978-1-59030-038-1
I. Chödzin, Sherab. II. Title.
PT2635.I65 V613 2003
833'.912—dc21
2002152897

My friend, once I put this book in your hands, and you were fonder of it than anyone before you. So I have become accustomed to thinking of it as belonging to you. Therefore, permit me, not only in your own book but in all the books of this new edition, to write your name, to write:

The *Stories of God* belong to Ellen Key.

Rainer Maria Rilke
Rome, April 1904

Contents

Stories of God

The Tale of God's Hands

One morning not long ago I ran into the lady next door. We exchanged greetings.

"What a fall!" she said after a moment and looked up into the sky. I did the same. For October it really was a clear and delicious morning. Suddenly, something occurred to me.

"What a fall!" I exclaimed, waving my hands about a little. My neighbor nodded in agreement. I watched her for a moment. Her good, wholesome face was moving up and down so sweetly. It was quite radiant; only around her lips and on her temples were there some little shadowy wrinkles. Where might those have come from?

And then, quite without warning, I asked her, "And your little girls?"

The wrinkles in her face vanished for a second but then immediately gathered again, even darker.

"They're in good health, thank God, only—" My neighbor set off down the street, and I now took up my place at her left side, in the proper manner. "You know, they're both now at an age, the children, where they ask questions all day long. What am I saying, 'all day long'—right on into the night!"

"Yes," I murmured, "there is a time—" But she paid me no heed.

"And not like: Where does this horse-trolley go? How many stars are there? And: Is ten thousand more than a lot? But quite different things: Does God speak Chinese too? And: What does God look like? Always all about God! But these are things we don't really know the answers to."

"No, of course not," I agreed. "We have certain ideas about them—"

"Or about God's hands. What are you supposed to—"

I looked my neighbor in the eyes. "Allow me," I said in a very polite manner. "The last thing you said was 'God's hands,' is that right?" She nodded. I think she was a little surprised. "Yes," I hastened to add, "the hands of God is something I do know a little about. By coincidence," I remarked quickly, as I saw her eyes begin to widen. "Entirely by coincidence . . . I just . . . well . . ." Then I concluded with resolve: "I will tell you what I know. If you have a minute, I'll keep you company on the way back to your house; that will be just enough time."

"Fine," she said, still surprised, when I finally let her get a word in. "But wouldn't you maybe want to tell—?"

"Tell the children myself? No, dear lady, that will not work, that simply will not work at all. You see, I immediately get embarrassed whenever I have to talk to children. That's not a bad thing in itself. But the children might take my confusion to mean I was lying to them. And since the truth of my story means a lot to me . . . You could retell it to them; you would do a much better job of it anyway. You could make it fit their understanding and embellish it a little. I'll just give you the simple facts in the shortest form. All right?"

"All right, all right," replied my neighbor, confused.

I thought for a moment: "In the beginning—" but then I broke off at once. "I can presume, my dear lady, that you already know much of what I'd have to tell the children first. For example, the Creation . . ." There was a rather long pause.

"Yes. And on the seventh day—" The good woman's voice was high and shrill.

"Stop!" I said. "We're going to want to keep the earlier days in mind too, aren't we? Because it mainly has to do with them. Well, anyway, God, as we know, began His work by making the earth, dividing it from the water, and ordaining light. Then, with remarkable speed, He formed things, I mean the big, substantial things that exist—rocks, mountains, a tree, and in the pattern of that one, many trees." At this point, I had already been hearing footsteps behind us for a while that were neither overtaking us nor falling behind either. That bothered me, and I got tangled up in my Creation story, continuing as follows: "You can only make this high-speed and productive activity understandable by assuming that, after long and deep reflection, everything was already completely ready in His head before He . . ."

Here the footsteps finally caught up with us, and a not particularly pleasant voice broke over us.

"Oh, you must be talking about Mr. Schmidt, excuse me. . . ."

I looked at the intruder with irritation, but my neighbor became very embarrassed.

"Ahem," she coughed. "No . . . that is . . . yes, we were just talking about, somehow about—"

"What a fall!" said the other woman suddenly, as if we'd had no exchange, and her small red face glowed.

"Yes," I heard my neighbor say. "You're right there, Mrs. Hüpfer, "an extraordinarily beautiful fall!"

Then the ladies parted. "And say hello to the children for me," Mrs. Hüpfer added with a giggle.

My good neighbor paid no further attention to her. After all, she was eager to hear my story. But, with incomprehensible harshness, I declared, "Yes, well! I've lost track of where we were."

"You were saying something about His head. That is . . ." The neighbor lady blushed very red.

I felt really sorry for her, so I quickly resumed my tale:

Yes, so you see, as long as only *things* were made, the dear Lord didn't have to keep His eye on the earth all the time. After all, nothing could happen there. The wind, it is true, was already blowing over the mountains, which were very much like the clouds that it was already familiar with, but it was still avoiding the treetops with a certain distrust. And that was fine with God. The *things* He had made in His sleep, so to speak. It was only when He began on the animals that the work started to interest Him. He bent over this work and only rarely raised His broad brows to cast a glance at the earth. He forgot it completely when He was forming human beings. I don't know what complicated part of the body He had come to when He heard a whirring of wings around Him.

An angel hurried past, singing, "Thou who seest everything. . . ."

God was startled. He had caused the angel to sin, for the latter had just sung a lie. Abruptly, God the Father looked down. And of course, something had already occurred down there that was going to be very difficult to make up for. A little bird was flying back and forth over the earth as though in fear, and God was not able to help it back home, because He had not seen what forest the poor creature had come out of. He became very angry and said: "The birds are supposed to stay where I put them." But then He remembered that, at the request of the angels, He had endowed them with wings, so that on earth too there would be something like the angels; and this circumstance upset Him even more.

Now, for such states of mind there is nothing so healing as work. And busy as He was with the fabrication of human beings, God quickly regained His happy state of mind. He had the eyes of the angel before Him as mirrors, and in them He took the measure of His own features and slowly and carefully formed, on a ball in His lap, the first face. He succeeded with the forehead. Much harder for Him was to make the two nostrils symmetrical. He bent ever further over this task, until there was again a movement of air round about Him. He looked up. The same angel was circling Him. This time no hymns were to be heard, for the youth had lost his voice as a result of his lie, but by looking at his mouth God could tell he was still singing, "Thou who seest everything." At once Saint Nicholas, who stood particularly high in God's esteem, approached Him and said through his great beard, "Thy lions are resting peacefully; they are very arrogant creatures, I must say! But a little dog is running around on the rim of the earth, a terrier; seest Thou, he's about to fall off." And in fact God did make out something bright and white, like a small light dancing to and fro in the vicinity of Scandinavia, where it is already so frightfully round. And He got very angry and told Saint Nicholas in no uncertain terms that if he wasn't satisfied with His lions, he should try making some himself. Whereupon Saint Nicholas departed from heaven, slamming the door and causing a star to fall right on the terrier's head.

Now the catastrophe was complete, and the dear Lord had to admit that He alone was to blame for everything, and He resolved nevermore to lift His gaze from the earth. And that is the way it has been. He left His work to His hands, which are of course also wise, and although He was highly curious to find out what the human being was going to end up looking like, He stared down unremittingly at the earth, on which now, as if to spite Him, not even a tiny leaf seemed to want to stir.

In order at least to reserve a small pleasure for Himself after all His trouble, He had commanded His hands to show Him the human being just before the time came for them to deliver it over into life. Again and again He asked, as children do when they are playing hide-and-seek, "Ready?" But all the answer He got was the sound of His hands kneading, and He waited. It seemed to Him quite a long time. Then, all at once, He saw something tumbling through space, something dark falling at such an angle that it seemed it had come from quite near Him. Filled with a dark premonition, He called for His hands.

They appeared, besmirched with clay and hot and quivering.

"Where is the human being?" He shouted at them. The right hand let fly at the left:

"You let him go!"

"Please!" said the left hand, incensed. "It was you who wanted to do everything by yourself—you wouldn't let me in on the business at all."

"You were the one who was supposed to hold him!" And the right hand wound up as if to strike. But then it thought better of it, and the hands, in their hurry to get in the next word, both said:

"He was so impatient, the human being. He kept wanting to be alive already. Neither one of us could do anything about it. Definitely, we are both innocent."

But the dear Lord was seriously angry. He pushed both hands away, for they were botching up His view of the earth, saying, "I know you no longer; do what you will." From that time on, the hands tried that, but no matter what they did, they could only begin things. Without God, there is no completion. And so they finally got tired of it. Now they spend the whole day kneeling, doing penance, or at least that's the story one hears. But the way it seems to us is that God rested because He was angry at His hands. So to this very moment we're still on the seventh day.

I remained silent for a moment. The neighbor lady took advantage of this to be very reasonable:

"And you think they'll never make up the quarrel?"

"Oh, yes," I said. "At least I hope so."

"And when will that be?"

"Well, not until God finds out what the human being His hands let go of against His will looks like."

My neighbor thought about this and then laughed: "But to do that, all He would have to do is look down."

"Excuse me," I said in a nice way, "your remark shows understanding, but my story isn't over yet. Well, so, by the time the hands had stepped aside and God was again surveying the earth, just about a minute had passed by, or let's say a millennium—which, as we know, amounts to the same thing. Instead of one human being there were now a million of them. But they were all already wearing clothes. And since the fashions of that particular time were especially ugly and also badly distorted people's faces, God got a completely false and (I won't gloss over it) a very bad impression of human beings."

"Hmm," said my neighbor, and wanted to say something more. But I ignored her and concluded with heavy emphasis:

"And for that reason it is urgently necessary for God to find out what human beings are really like. We should be happy that there are those of us who are able to tell Him."

But my neighbor was not happy. "And who would that be?"

"Why, quite simply the children, and maybe also anyone who paints, writes poems, and builds—"

"Builds what? Churches?"

"Yes, and other things, whatever—"

My neighbor slowly shook her head. A lot of what I'd said struck her as very odd indeed. We had already passed her house and now slowly turned around. Suddenly she became quite gay and laughed:

"But what nonsense! Of course God is omniscient. He must have known, for example, where the little bird had come from." She looked at me with an air of triumph. I was a little confused, I must admit. But once I had gotten hold of myself, I succeeded in putting on a very serious face.

"Dear lady," I lectured her, "in fact that is a story all by itself. But just so you won't think that's only an excuse on my part"—naturally at this point she protested strongly—"I will just say briefly: Of course, God has all the attributes. But before He was in a position, as it were, to apply them to the world, they all seemed to Him like one single big power. I don't know if I'm expressing myself clearly. But in relation to things, His powers became specialized and turned into duties to a certain extent. It was hard for Him to keep track of everything. You see, there are conflicts. (By the way, I'm telling all this only to you, and you are by no means to pass it along to the children.)"

"You don't have to worry about that," protested my listener.

"You see, if an angel had flown by and sung, 'Thou who *knowest* everything,' then everything would have been fine."

"And then there would have been no need for this story."

"Definitely," I confirmed. And I prepared to take my leave.

"But are you absolutely sure about all this?"

"Absolutely sure," I replied almost formally.

"Then I'll have to tell the children this today!"

"I would love to be able to listen in. Goodbye, then."

"Goodbye," she replied. Then she turned back again:

"But why was it this particular angel who—"

"My dear neighbor," I interrupted her, "I perceive that your two little girls don't ask so many questions just because they're children."

"Then why do they?" asked my neighbor, curious.

"Well, the doctors say there are certain hereditary traits. . . ." My neighbor wagged her finger at me. But all the same we parted good friends.

The next time I ran into my dear neighbor (which was, by the way, a fairly long time later), she was not alone, so I could not find out whether she had told her girls my story or how it had turned out. I was relieved of this uncertainty by a letter that I received shortly thereafter. Since I have not received the permission of the sender to make it public, I will have to confine myself to telling how it ended; this should make it fairly easy to figure out who it came from. It ended with the words: "Me and five other children, since I am one of them."

Immediately on receiving it, I answered as follows:

Dear Children,

It makes me happy to think that you enjoyed the tale of God's hands. I like it too. However, despite that, I cannot come pay you a visit. Do not be angry at me for this. Who knows if you would like me. I do not have a nice nose, and if—which happens from time to time—it also had a little red pimple on the end, you would spend the whole time looking and marveling at this little spot and would not hear at all what was being said just a short distance below. You would probably also dream about this little pimple. All this would not make me at all happy. Therefore, I suggest another way around the problem. We have (even besides your mother) a large number of friends and acquaintances in common who are not children. You will find out soon enough who. From time to time, I will tell them a story, and you will get a much nicer version from these intermediaries than I could ever come up with myself. For there are some great writers among these friends of ours. I will not tell you in advance what my stories will be about. But because nothing is more on your minds and in your hearts than the dear Lord, I will take every opportunity to fit in what I know about Him. If you find anything wrong, write me another nice letter, or have your mother tell me. For it is possible that I might make mistakes about a number of things, because it has been so long since I heard the most beautiful stories, and in the meantime have had to hear a lot that were not so beautiful. That is the way life goes. But nevertheless, life is a marvelous thing—that will often come up in my stories too. And so I remain

Yours Truly,
Me, but also just one more,
because I too am one of you.

The Stranger

A stranger wrote me a letter. The stranger wrote me not about Europe, not about Moses, not about either the major or minor prophets, not about the emperor of Russia or about Czar Ivan the Terrible, his fearsome forefather. Not about the mayor or the neighborhood shoe repairman, not about the nearby city nor about any distant city; nor were the woods full of deer that I get lost in every morning mentioned in his letter. He also told me nothing about his mother or his sisters, who are certainly long since married. Perhaps his mother is dead too—how can it be otherwise when I don't find her mentioned anywhere in a letter four pages long? He places a far greater trust in me: he treats me like his brother, he tells me his troubles.

In the evening the stranger pays me a visit. I do not light a lamp. I help him off with his coat and ask him to join me for tea, because it is just the time that I take my tea every day. In the case of such intimate visits, there is no need to place constraints on oneself. As we are about to sit down at the table, I notice that my guest is restless; his face is full of fear and his hands are shaking.

"Right," I say; "here's a letter for you." At that point I am ready to pour the tea. "Do you take sugar? Lemon, maybe? I learned to drink tea with lemon in Russia. Would you like to try it?" Then I light a lamp and place it somewhat high in a distant corner, so that the twilight actually still remains in the room; but now it is a warmer twilight than before, a bit rosy. And then the face of my guest begins to look a bit more confident, warmer, and much more familiar to me. I greet him once more with the words: "You know, I've been expecting you for a long time." And before the stranger has time to be surprised, I explain to him. "I know a story that I can tell to no one but you. Don't ask me why. Just tell me if you're comfortable in your chair, if the tea is sweet enough, and if you want to hear the story."

My guest had to smile. Then he answered simply: "Yes."

"Yes to all three?"

"To all three."

We both leaned back in our chairs at the same time, so that our faces fell into shadow. I put down my tea glass, took pleasure in the golden glow of the tea, slowly forgot this pleasure, and suddenly asked, "Do you still remember God?"

The stranger thought about this. His eyes peered off into the darkness, so that with the small points of light in the pupils they looked like two leaf-sheltered allées in a park, above which shone bright, open summer and sun. These, too, then, beginning thus as dim rounds, extended in ever-narrowing darkness to a single glimmering point—the exit on the far side into perhaps much brighter daylight. As I was watching this, he said hesitantly, as though he were using his voice only reluctantly:

"Yes, I still remember God."

"Good," I thanked him, "because it just so happens that my story is about Him. But first tell me one more thing. Do you ever talk to children?"

"It does happen, in passing at least."

"Perhaps you are already aware of the fact that, as a result of some ugly insubordination on the part of His hands, God doesn't know what the finished human being actually looks like?"

"I once heard that somewhere, I no longer know from whom," replied my guest. And I saw vague recollections chasing each other across his brow.

"It doesn't matter," I interrupted him, "just listen."

For a long time, God put up with this uncertainty. For His patience is as great as His strength. But once, when thick clouds had been hanging between Him and the earth for days at a time, with the result that He no longer knew whether He might have just dreamed everything—the world and people and time—He called for His right hand, which for so long had been banished and hidden away in small, trivial tasks. It hurried eagerly to Him, for it thought that God finally wanted to forgive it. When God saw it before Him in its beauty, youth, and strength, He was in truth inclined to forgive it. But just in time, He remembered Himself and commanded without looking at it:

"Go down onto the earth. Take the form that you see humans have, and position yourself on top of a mountain, naked, so that I can get a good look at you. As soon as you arrive down there, go to a young woman and tell her, but very softly, 'I want to live.' First you will be surrounded by a small darkness and then by a greater darkness, which is known as childhood, and then you will become a man and climb up the mountain, as I have just commanded you. The whole thing will only last a moment. Fare thee well."

The right hand said goodbye to the left hand, calling it by many nice names, and it has even been said that it suddenly bowed down to it and said, "O, thou holy spirit." But just then Saint Paul came along and lopped off God's right hand, and an archangel caught it and carried it off under his ample robe. God used His left hand to staunch the wound so that his blood would not stream down over the stars and fall in sad drops onto the earth.

A short time later, God, who was attentively following all the activities going on below, noticed that human beings wearing iron clothes were making a much greater fuss around one particular mountain than around any of the other mountains. And he expected to see His hand climbing up on top of it. But all that appeared was a man in what looked like a red cloak lugging something black that swayed from side to side. At the same moment, God's left hand, which lay over His open wound, began to get restless, and all at once, before God could stop it, it quit its place and began flitting about like a mad thing among the stars, crying: "Oh, poor right hand, and I can't do a thing to help it!" At the same time it began tugging on God's left arm, to the lower end of which it was attached, trying to pull itself loose. But the whole of the earth was red with God's blood, and there was no way of seeing what was going on down there. God almost died that time. With His last strength, He called His right hand back. Pale and trembling, it returned and lay down in its place like a sick animal. But even the left hand, which already knew quite a bit, since it had seen the right hand of God back there on the earth as it was scaling the mountain in the red cloak, was unable to find out from it the rest of what had taken place on that mountain. It must have been something very terrible. For God's right hand has still not recovered from it, and it has suffered from its memories not less than from the wrath of God, who after all had yet to forgive His hands.

My voice took a little rest. The stranger had covered his face with his hands. Things stayed like that for a long time. Then the stranger, in a voice that I had long since recognized, said,

"And why did you tell *me* this story?"

"Who else would have understood me? You come to me without rank, without office, without honors and distinctions, almost without a name. It was dark when you came in, but all the same I detected a resemblance in your features."

The stranger looked up at me questioningly.

"Yes," I replied to his silent look, "I often think, maybe God's hand is again off on its mission."

The children ended up hearing this story, and evidently it was told to them in such a way that they could understand it. For they are very fond of this story.

Why the Dear Lord Wants There to Be Poor People

The foregoing story had circulated so widely that our worthy schoolteacher was walking around the streets with a hurt look on his face. I find this quite understandable. It is bad for a teacher when the children suddenly know something he has not told them. The teacher has to be the only hole in the plank through which you can see into the orchard. If there are other holes there, the children crowd around a new one every day and soon get tired of the view altogether. I would not have used this comparison here, since perhaps not every teacher would go along with being a hole; but the teacher I am talking about, who is my neighbor, heard the comparison from me first and deemed it a highly accurate one. And in case somebody else has another view on this, for me my neighbor's authority is definitive.

He stood before me, toying constantly with his spectacles, and said, "I don't know who told the children this story, but in any case, it is not right to fill their imaginations with these unusual kinds of notions and get them all excited. We're dealing here with a kind of fairy tale—"

"By chance I happened to hear it," I interrupted him.

"So," said the teacher, who found this not at all improbable, "what do you think about it?" I hesitated, and he continued quickly, "To begin with, I find it improper to make free and unauthorized use of religious, especially biblical, material. All those things are, in any case, described in the catechism in such a way that they couldn't be better expressed." I wanted to say something but remembered just in time that the teacher had said "to begin with," which, according to grammar and for the sake of the health of the sentence, would have to be followed by a "then" and maybe even by an "and finally" before I could permit myself to interject anything. And indeed, that is what happened. Since our worthy schoolteacher also passed along this sentence, whose flawless construction would not fail to charm any connoisseur, to other people as well, and since they are no more likely to forget it than I am, I shall record here what came, just like the finale of an overture, after those lovely preparatory words "and finally":

"And finally, leaving aside the highly fantastical aspect of it, it seems to me that the material has been nowhere near adequately thought through nor considered from every angle. If I had time to write stories—"

"You find something missing in the story as we've heard it?"

"Yes, I find a great deal missing. From the literary-critical point of view, as it were. If I may speak to you as a colleague—"

I didn't know what he was talking about, and humbly said, "You're too kind, but I've never done any teaching—" Suddenly, something occurred to me. I broke off and he continued somewhat coolly:

"Just to mention one thing, it cannot be assumed (if we're going to go into the meaning of the story that deeply) that God . . . that God . . . well, I mean . . . that God should have made no further attempt to see human beings as they are, that is—"

At this point I felt the time had come to placate our worthy schoolteacher. I bowed slightly and began:

"We all know that you have passionately espoused (and, if I may say so, not without encountering a certain reciprocal warmth) the study of social questions." Our worthy schoolteacher smiled. "Well, so then I may assume that what I am thinking of sharing with you in a moment will not be entirely alien to your interests, especially since this will allow me to respond to your last insightful remark." He looked at me with amazement.

"You mean that God—"

"Precisely," I confirmed. "God is even now in the process of making a fresh attempt."

"Really?" the teacher snapped. "Are the authorities aware of this?"

"I can't provide you with precise information about that," I lamented. "I'm not in contact with those circles, but would you perhaps still like to hear my little story?"

"I would consider it a great favor." The teacher removed

his spectacles and painstakingly cleaned the lenses, leaving his naked eyes bashfully exposed.

I began.

Once the dear Lord was looking down into a big city. When the pandemonium He encountered had tired His eyes (the power system with its electric wires had a lot to do with this), He decided to confine His gaze to a single tall apartment building for a while, because this cost Him a lot less effort. At the same time, He remembered His old desire just once to see a living human being, and with this purpose His gaze entered the windows of the various stories, rising floor by floor. The people on the first floor (a rich businessman and his family) were almost entirely clothing. Not only were all parts of their bodies covered with expensive fabrics, but the outer silhouette of these clothes displayed a form in various places such that no body could possibly be underneath. On the second floor, things were not much better. And the people living three flights up had significantly less clothing on, it is true, but they were so dirty that the dear Lord could see only gray creases and in His goodness was almost ready to command these to become fruitful. At last, under the roof, in a crooked little room, God found a man in a coat of bad quality who was busy kneading clay.

"Oho, where did you get that?" He called to him.

The man, without bothering to take his pipe out of his mouth, growled: "The devil knows where. I wish I had become a shoemaker. Here I sit, working away . . ." And no matter what the dear Lord asked him, the man hung onto his bad humor and gave no further reply. Until, one day, he got a big letter from the mayor of that city. After that, he told God everything, without having to be asked. He had gone so long without getting a commission. Now, all of a sudden, he was supposed to make a statue for the main city park, and it was supposed to be called *The Truth.* The artist worked night and day in a distant studio, and various old memories came back to the dear Lord as He watched this. If He had not still been angry at His hands, He might also have started on some work. But the very day the statue called *The Truth* was to be carried out to its place in the park garden, where God too would have been able to see it in all its completeness, a huge scandal broke out, for a committee made up of city fathers, teachers, and other influential personalities had demanded that the statue be partially clothed before being exhibited to the public. The artist was cursing so loudly God could not make out what the trouble was. The city fathers, teachers, and the others had brought him to this sin, and God was surely going to avenge. . . .

"But you're coughing terribly!"

"It will pass," said the teacher in a perfectly clear voice. "Well, I have only a little more to report."

The dear Lord loosed His hold on that apartment building and that city park and was intending to pull His gaze back altogether, as a man pulls his fishing lure out of the water with one jerk to see if anything has bitten or not. In this case, there was actually something hanging there:

a very small house with several human beings inside who all had very little on because they were very poor. "So that's it," God thought; "the people have to be poor. I think these here are already quite poor, but I am going to make them so poor that they won't even have a shirt on their backs." That was the dear Lord's plan.

❧

Here I put a sound of finality in my voice in order to indicate that I had come to the end. The worthy schoolteacher was not satisfied with this. He found this story just as inconclusive and insufficiently rounded off as the previous one. "Yes," I excused myself, "a writer will have to come along who can invent some sort of a fantastic ending for the story, because in very truth, it doesn't have an ending yet."

"What do you mean?" said the schoolteacher, eyeing me in suspense.

"But, dear teacher," I reminded him, "how forgetful you are! You yourself are on the executive committee of the local association for the poor."

"Yes, I've been on it for about ten years and—"

"That's precisely the point. For the longest time you and your association have been preventing God from achieving His goal. You give people clothes."

"But please," the teacher said humbly, "that is nothing more than loving one's neighbor. And that, after all, pleases God to the highest degree."

"I see. And are the authorities fully convinced of this?" I asked guilelessly.

"Of course we are. I myself, in my capacity as member of

the executive committee of the association for the poor, have heard many words of praise. Just between us, the next time promotions come up, for my work in this regard . . . you understand?" The worthy teacher blushed bashfully.

"I wish you all the best," I replied. We shook hands, and the worthy schoolteacher departed with such a proud and measured gait that I am sure he was late for school.

As I later heard, the children did come to know part of this story (the part that is suitable for children). Could it be that the worthy schoolteacher composed an ending for it?

How Treachery Came to Russia

I have another friend here in the neighborhood. He's a blond man who is crippled and keeps his chair right up by the window both winter and summer. He can look very young; indeed his attentive face often has something boyish about it. But there are also days when he ages, the minutes pass over him like years, and suddenly he is an old man whose dull eyes have lost nearly all their life. We have known each other for a long time. At first we always exchanged glances, later we smiled involuntarily, we said hello to each other for a year, and since God knows when we have been telling each other this and that, unselectively, just as it comes up.

"Hello there," he called out as I was passing by and his window was still open to let in the rich, quiet autumn. "I haven't seen you for a long time."

"Hello, Ewald." I went up to his window as I usually did when I went by. "I took a trip."

"Where did you go?" he asked with impatience in his eyes.

"To Russia."

"Oh, as far as that." He leaned back and then said, "What sort of a country is it, Russia? A very large one, right?"

"Yes," I said, "it's big, and not only that—"

"Was that a stupid question?" Ewald smiled, turning red.

"No, Ewald. Quite the contrary. Your asking what sort of a country it is makes a number of things clear to me. For example, what Russia is bounded by."

"On the east?" my friend interjected.

I thought for a minute. "No."

"On the north?" the handicapped man pressed me.

Then I realized something. "Don't you see," I said, "looking at maps has spoiled people. There everything is level and flat, and when they've located things in terms of directions, they think that's all there is to it. But a country is not an atlas. It has mountains and gorges. So of course it must touch on something both above and below."

"Hmm," my friend reflected. "You're right. What could Russia border on, on those two sides?" Suddenly the ailing man looked like a little boy.

"You know!" I cried.

"On God, maybe?"

"Yes," I confirmed, "on God."

"I see," my friend nodded, full of understanding. Only then did a doubt enter his mind. "Is God a country, then?"

"I don't think so," I replied, "but in primitive languages many things have the same name. There is certainly a kingdom called God, and the ruler of it is also called God. Simple folk often can't distinguish between their country and their emperor; both are big and kind, frightening and big."

"I understand," said the man at the window slowly. "And do the people in Russia notice this nearness?"

"They take notice of it every chance they get. The influence of God is very powerful. No matter what people bring there from Europe, objects from the West become stones as soon as they cross the border. They might be precious stones, but just for the rich people, the so-called educated; but the bread the people live on comes from over there in that other kingdom."

"So the people must have more than they need of that."

I hesitated. "No, that's not the way it is. Certain circumstances make the imports from God difficult." I tried to draw him away from this thought. "But people have taken over many of the customs from that vast neighboring country. The whole style of ceremonies, for example. People speak to the czar as though to God."

"So people don't say, 'Your Majesty'?"

"No, they call them both 'little father.'"

"And people kneel to both of them?"

"People prostrate full length on the ground before both of them; they touch the ground with their foreheads and cry and say, 'I have sinned, forgive me, little father.' The Germans who see that call it a completely undignified form of slavery. I have a different view about it. What does kneeling mean? It has the sense of saying, 'I am in awe.' The Germans feel that, to express that, it is enough merely to remove their hats. Well, now, the salute, the bow, are both also more or less ways of expressing the same thing. They're abbreviations that have come about in countries where there was not enough room for everybody to lie down full length on the ground. But abbreviations are just used mechanically, without people any longer being aware of their meaning. For that reason, it's a good idea, wherever there's still space and time for it, to spell out the whole gesture—the whole beautiful and important word *awe.*"

"Yes, if I could, I would kneel down too," the crippled man dreamed.

"But in Russia," I continued after a pause, "many other things also come from God. There is the feeling that everything new is introduced by Him; every article of clothing, every food, every virtue, and even every sin first has to have His approval before it comes into use." The ailing man looked at me almost in fear. "This is only a fairy tale I'm referring to," I hastened to calm him down, "a so-called *bylina*,* a 'bygone' we could call it. I'll give you the gist of it in a few words. The title is 'How Treachery Came to Russia.'"

I leaned against the window frame, and the crippled man closed his eyes, which he liked to do whenever a story began.

> The terrible czar Ivan wanted to impose tribute on the neighboring princes and threatened them with a great war unless they sent gold to Moscow, the White City. The princes, after taking counsel, said as one man: "We shall give you three riddles. Come on the day that we indicate to the east, to the white stone, where we shall be assembled, and tell us the three answers. If they are right, we shall immediately give you the twelve casks of gold you demand from us."
>
> Czar Ivan Vassilievitch set to pondering, but the many bells of his broad white city, Moscow, disturbed him. Then he called his learned men and counselors to him,

---

*A *bylina* (plural, *bylini*) is a legend or oral epic of Russian literature.—Ed.

and one by one he had those who could not answer the questions simply taken out onto the large red square (where just then the church dedicated to Vassily the Naked was being built) and beheaded. With this keeping him busy, the time passed by so quickly for him that he suddenly found himself on the way to the east, to the white stone where the princes were waiting. He had no answer to any of the three questions, but the ride ahead of him was long, and there was still the possibility he might meet a wise man; for in those days there were many wise men on the roads as refugees, since all the kings were in the habit of cutting off their heads whenever they did not seem to be wise enough. As it happened, he failed to encounter such a person. But one morning he saw an old bearded peasant who was building a church. He had already gotten as far as the framework for the roof and was putting the small slats in place on top of it. And it was quite curious to see how the old peasant kept climbing down off the church again and again to fetch the narrow slats one by one from where they were piled up below, instead of taking a bunch of them along all at once in his long caftan. Because of this he was constantly obliged to climb up and down, and it seemed by no means unlikely that he was going to carry each one of the many hundred slats to its place in this manner. This made the czar impatient.

"Idiot!" he shouted (that is what peasants are usually called in Russia), "you should take a full load of your wood pieces and then climb back up on top of the church; that would be a lot simpler."

The peasant, who just at that moment was on the

ground, stopped where he was, put his hand up above his eyes, and replied: "You'll have to leave that to me, Czar Ivan Vassilievitch; each person understands his own craft the best. In the meantime, since you happen to be riding by, I'll tell you the answers to the three riddles that you'll need to know when you get to the white stone, which is not at all far from here." And he drilled him in the three answers, one after the other. The czar was so astounded he could hardly thank him.

"What should I give you as a reward?" he finally asked.

"Not a thing," said the peasant, and he started to climb back up his ladder.

"Stop!" the czar commanded. "That is unacceptable; you have to tell me your wish."

"Well, little father, if you command it, give me one of the twelve casks of gold that you will receive from the princes in the east."

"Fine," the czar agreed. "I'll give you a cask of gold." Then he rode off in haste so he would not forget the answers.

Later, when the czar came back from the east with his twelve casks of gold, he shut himself up in Moscow in his palace, in the very heart of the five-towered Kremlin, and poured out one cask after the other over the shining tiles of the hall, making a veritable mountain of gold, which cast a big black shadow over the floor. In his forgetfulness, the czar had also emptied the twelfth cask. He was about to fill it back up, but it was painful for him to have to take away so much gold from the magnificent pile. In the night, he went down into the courtyard, scooped fine sand into the cask until it was three-quarters full, crept stealthily back into the palace, and covered the sand with gold. The next morning he sent the cask with a messenger to the region of great Russia where the peasant was building his church.

When the peasant saw the messenger coming, he climbed down from the roof and cried, "You must come no closer, my friend. Go back and take your cask with you. Its contents are three-quarters sand and barely a quarter gold. I don't need it. Tell your master that until now there's been no treachery in Russia. But he himself is to blame if he should look around him now and see that there's no one he can trust. For he has just illustrated how one man betrays another, and century after century, his example will be emulated by many people throughout Russia. I don't need his gold; I can live without gold. It wasn't gold I was looking to him for, but truth and righteousness. But he cheated me. Tell that to your master, the terrible czar Ivan Vassilievitch, who resides in his white city of Moscow with a bad conscience and a golden robe."

After riding for a time, the messenger turned back. The peasant and his church had vanished. And also the heap of slats was no longer there—there was nothing there but empty, level ground. Then the man, shocked and horrified, stormed back to Moscow, stood breathless before the czar, and recounted to him in a scarcely understandable manner what had happened, saying that the supposed peasant could have been none other than God Himself.

"Do you think he was right?" my friend wondered softly, after my story had died away on the air.

"Maybe," I replied, "but, you know, people are . . . superstitious . . . and on top of that, I have to go now, Ewald."

"That's a pity," said the crippled man in a heartfelt manner. "Will you tell me another story again soon?"

"Gladly, but under one condition," I said, moving back toward the window.

"And that is?" said Ewald, surprised.

"From time to time, you have to retell them all to the children in the neighborhood," I requested.

"Oh, the children come and visit me so rarely nowadays."

"They'll come," I consoled him. "Evidently you haven't wanted to tell them any stories lately, and perhaps you haven't had any subject matter—or too much subject matter. But when somebody knows a real story, do you really think that can stay hidden? Watch out, the word spreads fast, especially among the children. Goodbye, now." And with that, I departed.

And the children heard the story the very same day.

How Old Timofei Died Singing

What a joy it is to tell stories to a handicapped person! Healthy people are so flighty; they look at things first from one side and then from another. And if you have been walking with them for an hour with them on your right, they might suddenly respond to you from the left, just because it has occurred to them that this might be more polite or show signs of a better upbringing. With a crippled person, you do not have to fear this. His immobility makes him more like a thing, and in fact he keeps up quite warm relations with things; it makes him, so to speak, into a thing that is quite superior to other things, one that listens not only with its silence but also with its rare, softly spoken words, and with its gentle, reverent feelings.

I like best telling stories to my friend Ewald. And I was very glad when he called to me from his everyday place at the window: "I have to ask you something."

Immediately I went over to him and gave him my greetings.

"Where does that story you recently told me come from?" he finally asked. "From a book?"

"Yes," I replied sadly, "the scholars buried it in there when it died; that's not long ago at all. It was still alive a hundred years ago, surely completely without a care and on many lips. But the words that people use nowadays, these heavy words that can't be sung, were hostile to it and took one mouth after another away from it, so that at the end it was eking out a very withdrawn and shabby existence on one dried-out pair of lips, like someone on a lowly widow's pension. That's where it died too, without leaving any posterity behind, and it was then, as we have already said, buried with all honors in a book, where others of its kin were already at rest."

"And was it very old when it died?" asked my friend, falling in with my drift.

"Four to five hundred years old," I reported quite truthfully, "and various of its relatives reached an even more advanced age."

"You mean, without ever being laid to rest in a book?"

"As far as I know, they were moving from one pair of lips to another the whole time."

"They didn't even take time off to sleep?"

"Oh, yes, immediately upon rising from the lips of a singer, they took up residence in a heart, where it was warm and dark."

"Were people so quiet, then, that songs could sleep in their hearts?" Ewald seemed quite incredulous.

"That must have been the case. It is said that they talked less, danced dances that rose slowly to a climax and had a nice swaying quality to them, and above all, they didn't laugh loudly the way we hear people doing today, in spite of the generally higher level of culture."

Ewald was just about to ask another question, but he thought better of it and smiled: "I keep asking one question after the other—but maybe you have a story in mind?" He looked at me with anticipation.

A story? Oh, I don't know. I only wanted to tell you that these songs were passed down in certain families. One generation took them and passed them on to the next, not entirely unused, showing the wear and tear of daily use, but nevertheless undamaged—somewhat the way old Bibles get passed down from grandparents to grandchildren. A disinherited person was distinguished from his fully entitled kin by the fact that he couldn't sing, or at least knew only a fraction of the songs of his fathers and grandfathers and had lost along with the rest of the songs that crucial body of experience that all these *bylini* and *skaski** represented for the people. Thus, for example, Yegor Timofeyevitch, against the will of his father, old Timofei, had married a beautiful young woman and moved with her to Kiev, the holy city, in the vicinity of which are the tombs of the greatest martyrs of the holy Orthodox Church. Father Timofei, known as the most accomplished singer for ten days' journey all around, cursed his son and told his neighbor that he often felt pretty sure he'd never had a son. Nevertheless, in his trouble and sorrow he became mute and turned away all the young people who crowded into his hut to receive

---

**Skaski* is Russian for "stories" or "fairy tales."—Ed.

the heritage of many songs that was shut up in the old man as in a dust-laden violin:

"Father, our little father, just sing us this or that song. You see, we want to take them back to our villages, and then you would hear them in all the yards as soon as evening came and the animals had settled down for the night."

The old man just kept sitting on the stove shaking his head the whole day long. He did not hear well anymore, and since he was never sure that one of the young people who were now always hovering around his house had not asked for a song again, he set his white head to shaking: no, no, no, until he fell asleep, and for a while longer afterward. He would have gladly satisfied the young people; it made him sad to think that maybe very soon his own mute, dead dust would lie over the songs. But if he had tried to teach something to one of the lads, then surely he would have had to remember his own Yegoruschka, and who knows what would have happened then! For only because he was altogether silent had no one ever seen him cry. For him, behind every word lay a sob, and he always had to be careful to keep his mouth closed, for otherwise, out they would have come.

Starting very early on, old Timofei had taught his only son, Yegor, songs one by one, and by the time the boy was five, he already knew how to sing more songs and how to sing them more accurately than all the grown-up youths in the village and the whole region around. All the same, mostly on holidays when he was a bit tipsy, the old man would say to the boy, "Yegoruschka, my little dove, I have already taught you to sing a lot of songs, many *bylini,* and also the legends of the saints—practically one for every day. But, as you know, I am the most accomplished singer in the whole province, and my father pretty well knew the songs of all of Russia and some Tatar stories into the bargain. You are still very young, and therefore I have not yet told you the most beautiful *bylini,* whose words are like icons and cannot be compared to ordinary words; and you have not yet learned those tunes that no one—be he Cossack or peasant—has ever been able to listen to without crying."

Timofei repeated this to his son every Sunday and on all of the many holidays of the Russian calendar—that is to say, fairly often. Until the son, after a passionate quarrel with the old man, immediately disappeared with beautiful Ustyenka, the daughter of a poor peasant.

The third year after this incident, Timofei fell ill, just as one of the many pilgrimages that are constantly being made from all parts of the vast country to Kiev was about to begin. At that time Ossip, his neighbor, appeared at the sick man's house.

"I'm going along with the pilgrims, Timofei Ivanovitch; allow me to embrace you one more time." Ossip was not particularly close to the old man, but now that he was about to set forth on a long journey, he found it necessary to take leave of him as of a father. "I have sometimes hurt your feelings," he blubbered; "forgive me, dear heart. It happened when I'd been drinking, and there is nothing one can do about that, as you know. So now I'm going to pray for you and light a candle for you. Farewell, Timofei Ivanovitch, my little father. Perhaps you'll get well again, God willing, and then you'll sing for us again.

Yes, yes, it's been a long time since you've sung for us. What songs those were! The one about Duke Stepanovitch, for example—do you think I've forgotten it? How stupid of you! I still know it very, very well. Of course, not like you—you really had it mastered, that we have to say. God gave you that; to others he gave other things. Me, for example . . ."

The old man, who lay on the stove, turned over, groaning, and made a movement as though he wanted to say something. It was as if one could hear very faintly the name Yegor. Maybe he wanted to send him a message. But when the neighbor asked him from the doorway, "Did you say something, Timofei Ivanovitch?" he was already lying there again quite quietly, and he shook his white head. Nevertheless, God knows how it happened, hardly a year after Ossip set out, Yegor returned home quite unexpectedly. The old man did not recognize him immediately, because it was dark in the hut, and the old eyes were reluctant to register a new, unfamiliar form. But when Timofei heard the stranger's voice, he was startled and jumped down off the stove on his wobbly old legs. Yegor caught him, and they held each other in their arms. Timofei wept. The young man asked him repeatedly, "Have you been sick long, father?" When the old man had calmed down a bit, he crawled back on top of the stove, and inquired in a different, stern tone of voice, "And your wife?" A pause. Then Yegor blurted out:

"I chased her away, you know, with the child." He was silent for a time. "One day Ossip came to see me. 'Ossip Nikiforovitch?' I said. 'Yes,' he said, 'it's me. Your father is sick, Yegor. He can't sing anymore. It is very quiet in the village, as if there wasn't a soul in it, our village. Nothing makes a noise, nothing moves, nobody cries anymore, and there's no real reason to laugh either.'

"I thought this over. What should be done? Then I called for my wife. 'Ustyenka,' I say, 'I have to go home, otherwise there will be nobody to sing there. It's my turn now. My father is sick.'

" 'Fine,' says Ustyenka.

" 'But I can't take you along,' I explain to her; 'my father, as you know, doesn't want you around. And also I probably won't come back to you once I'm there and singing.' Ustyenka understands me.

" 'So then, God be with you. There are many pilgrims here now, and so there are alms aplenty. God will help, Yegor.' And so I set out. And now, father, tell me all your songs."

The word spread that Yegor was back and that old Timofei was singing again. But that autumn the wind blew so fiercely through the village that no one who passed by could say for sure if there was singing going on in Timofei's house or not. And the door was opened to no one who knocked. The two of them wanted to be alone. Yegor sat on the edge of the stove his father was lying on and from time to time would bring his ear right up to the old man's mouth. For the old man was truly singing. His old voice, faltering and quaking a little, carried to Yegor all the most beautiful songs, and the son from time to time rocked his head back and forth or swung his legs hanging down over the side of the stove just as though he were singing himself.

For many days it went on like this. Timofei kept finding a more beautiful song in his memory. Often at night he woke his son, and making vague movements with his withered, restless hands, he would sing a little song and then another and then another—till sluggish morning reluctantly began to stir. Shortly after the most beautiful song, he died. During the last days he had sorely complained again and again that he still had an untold number of songs in him but no longer had the time to share them all with his son. He lay there with furrowed brow, in the throes of strenuous, anxious reflection, and his lips quivered with anticipation. From time to time he sat up, rocked his head back and forth for a while, moved his lips, and then finally some faint song came through. But now for the most part he sang the same stanzas of Duke Stepanovitch that were his favorites, and his son, in order to keep him from getting angry, had to let on that he was surprised and that he was hearing them for the first time.

After old Timofei died, the house, in which Yegor now lived by himself, remained shut up for a period of time. Then, in the early spring, Yegor Timofeyevitch, who now had a rather long beard, came out the door and began pacing back and forth in the village and singing. Later he went to the neighboring villages as well, and the peasants began telling one another that Yegor had turned into at least as accomplished a singer as his father, Timofei. For he knew a great number of grave and heroic songs and those tunes that no one—be he Cossack or peasant—could listen to without breaking into tears. And on top of that, it was said, he sang with a sad and tender tone such as had never been heard from any singer. And this tone always appeared quite expectedly in the refrain, where it had a particularly moving effect.

"So he didn't learn this tone from his father?" said my friend Ewald after a while.

"No," I replied, "no one knows where it came from." After I had already taken a few steps away from the window, the crippled man called after me:

"Maybe he was thinking about his wife and his child. By the way, did he never send for them, even after his father died?"

"No, I don't think so. At least he later died alone."

The Song of Justice

The next time I passed by Ewald's window, he waved me over and smiled. "Did you promise the children something specific?"

"What do you mean?" I said, surprised.

"Well, when I told the story about Yegor, they complained that God did not appear in the story." I was stunned.

"What? A story without God? How is that possible?" Then I reflected. "It's true, actually, when I think about it now, the story doesn't say anything about God. I don't understand how that could have happened. If somebody had requested such a story, I think I could have thought about it my whole life through without coming up with one—"

My friend smiled at this heated response. "You shouldn't excite yourself about it," he interrupted me in a kindly sort of a way. "My own view is that you can never know whether or not God is in a story until you get all the way to the end. For if only two words are still missing, yes, even if the pause after the final words still hasn't occurred, He can always still show up." I nodded, and the crippled man said in another tone of voice, "Don't you know something more about these Russian singers?"

I hesitated. "Yes, well, wouldn't we rather just talk about God, Ewald?"

He shook his head. "I'd like so much to hear more about these remarkable men. I don't know how it happens, but I'm always thinking, if one of them were to come here to my place . . ." and he turned his head toward the interior of the room, toward the door. But then his eyes turned back to me, not without embarrassment, "But that is of course not possible," he chastened himself hurriedly.

"Why shouldn't it be possible, Ewald? A lot could happen to you that is impossible for people who can use their legs, because they pass by so many things and run away from so much. God has destined you, Ewald, to be a still point in the midst of all the rushing around. Don't you feel how everything revolves around you? Other people run after their days, and when they have at last for once caught up with one, they are so breathless that they can't talk with it at all. But you, my friend, simply sit at your window and wait; and something always comes to him who waits. You have a very special fate. Just think, even the Iberian Madonna in Moscow has to leave her little chapel and ride in her black carriage with four horses to whoever is having a ceremony, whether it is for a baptism or a death. But in your case, everything must come to you."

"Yes," said Ewald with a strange smile, "I can't even go to meet Death. Many people run into him when they're out going places. He is afraid to enter their houses and draws them out into alien territory, away to a war, to a precipitous tower, to a wobbly bridge, out into the wilderness, or into insanity. Most people pick him up, at least, outside somewhere and then carry him home on their shoulders without realizing it. For Death is sluggish and lazy; if people weren't continually prodding at him, who knows, he might fall asleep." The ailing man thought awhile about this and then continued with a certain pride, "But in my case, he will have to come to me. Here to my little sunny room, where flowers last so long, over this old carpet, past this cabinet, between the table and the end of the bed (it isn't that easy to get by), all the way here, to my dear, old, roomy chair, which will probably die along with me, since it has, in a manner of speaking, lived with me. And he will have to do all that in the normal, accepted manner, without making a fuss, without knocking anything over, without doing anything out of the ordinary, just like anyone paying a visit. This makes me feel oddly close to my room. Everything will play out here, on this narrow stage, and for that reason even this final incident will not be very different from all the others that have taken place here and will in the future. It has always seemed strange to me, even when I was a child, that people talk about death in a different way than they do about anything else; and the only reason for that is, nobody who dies tells us anything about what happened to him afterward.

"But what makes a dead person different from someone who becomes serious, turns away from the passing scene, and goes into seclusion to quietly consider the answer to something that has tormented him for a long time? In the midst of people, you can't even remember the Lord's Prayer, much less a certain ominous subject that perhaps is made up not of words but of events. A person has to go off somewhere into an inaccessible, silent place—and maybe the dead are people who have withdrawn from everything in order to reflect upon life."

A silence followed, which I rounded off with the following words: "That makes me think of a certain young girl. It could be said that in the first seventeen years of her life, all she had done was look. Her eyes were such big, independent things that they themselves used up everything they took in, and the life in the rest of the young creature's body went on quite apart from them, nourished by its own simple inner movements. But at the end of this time some overly intense event disturbed this double life, the two aspects of which were scarcely in contact with each other. It was as though her eyes broke through to the inside of her and the whole weight of the outside world tumbled down through them into her dark heart; and each day crashed with such force down those deep, precipitous shafts of sight that it broke to pieces like a glass in her narrow chest. The young girl lost her color, became sickly and solitary, began to think, and finally sought out for herself that stillness where, hopefully, one's thoughts are no longer disturbed."

"How did she die?" asked my friend softly, in a slightly hoarse voice.

"She drowned. In a deep, still pond, and on its surface there arose many rings that slowly broadened and spread in among the white water lilies, causing all those waterborne blossoms to bob up and down."

"Is that a story?" asked Ewald, in order to avoid being overwhelmed by the silence behind my words.

"No," I replied, "that's a feeling."

"But couldn't one also convey that to the children?"

I thought about it. "And by what means?"

"By means of another story."

And I began to tell it. "It was during the time that the people of southern Russia were fighting for their freedom."

"Excuse me," said Ewald. "What do you mean by that? Do you mean that the people were trying to get free of the czar? That wouldn't fit with the way I think of Russia, and would also conflict with your own earlier stories. In this case I would rather not hear your story, because I like the picture I have created for myself of things there, and I'd like to keep it intact."

I had to smile. Reassuringly I told him:

The Polish *pans* (I should have told you this to begin with) were lords in southern Russia and in those silent, lonely steppes that are known as the Ukraine. Their oppression and the greed of the Jews—who even held the keys to the churches, which they gave out to the Orthodox believers only for a fee—had made the young people around Kiev and all the way up the Dnieper weary and thoughtful.

The city itself, Kiev the Holy, the place where Russia first showed itself in its four hundred domed church towers, sank ever more into itself and was consumed by fires as by sudden insane thoughts—behind which the night only became ever more boundless. The people of the steppe did not clearly know what was happening. But seized by a strange restlessness, the old men came out of their huts at night and silently contemplated the eternal windless heavens, and by day figures could be seen appearing on the tops of the *kurgans*, where they stood outlined against the distant flatness. These *kurgans* are the burial places of long-gone tribes that are strewn over the length and breadth of the plain like frozen, sleeping waves. And in this land, where the graves are the mountains, the people are the abysses. Deep, dark, and silent are these people, and their words are no more than weak, unsteady bridges over their true beings.

Sometimes dark birds rise from the *kurgans.* Sometimes wild songs plunge into the darkening people and disappear deep within them, as the birds disappear into the far reaches of the sky. In all directions, everything seems endless. The very houses cannot provide a shield against this immensity; their small windows are filled with it. Only in the dark corners of the rooms the old icons stand like milestones of God, and the shimmer of a small light passes through their frames like a lost child through the starry night. These icons are the sole reference point, the only reliable signpost along the way, and no house can exist without them. New ones are always needed—when one falls apart from age or decay, when someone gets married and builds a new hut, or when somebody—for example, old Abraham—dies with the desire to take Saint Nicholas, the wonder-worker, along with him in his hands joined in prayer, doubtless so he can compare the saints in heaven with this picture and acknowledge this most highly venerated one above all the others.

This is how it happens that Peter Akimovitch, though really a shoemaker by trade, also paints icons. When he is tired of one kind of work, he changes over, after having crossed himself three times, to the other one, and over both his sewing and hammering and his painting the same piety presides. By now he is already an old man, but fairly vigorous nonetheless. His back, which he bends over his boots, he straightens up again when he paints, and thus he has maintained good posture and a certain balance in his shoulders and lower back. He has spent the better part of his life entirely alone, not getting in the least involved in the turmoil that came about when his wife Akulina bore him children and when these died or got married. Only in his seventieth year did Peter begin to relate to those who remained in the house and to regard them as really and truly there.

They were Akulina, his wife, a quiet, humble person, who had spent herself almost to the dregs on her children; an aging, ugly daughter; and Alyosha, a son who had been born inordinately late and was just seventeen years old. Peter wanted to train Alyosha to paint; for he saw that before long he would not be able to fill all the orders that were coming in. But he soon dropped the lessons. Alyosha had painted the Holy Virgin but had come up with something so far from the strict and proper paragon that his concoction looked like a picture of Mariana, the daughter of the cossack Golokopytenko, that is to say, like something thoroughly sinful; and old Peter, having crossed himself, hastened to paint over the offending board with a picture of Saint Dimitri, who for unknown reasons he prized above all the other saints.

Alyosha also did not try to paint any more pictures. When his father had not ordered him to gild a halo, he was usually out on the steppes, no one knew where. No one kept him at home. The mother was bewildered by him and was shy of talking to him, as if he were a stranger or an official. His sister had beaten him while he was still a child, and now, since Alyosha had grown up, she had begun to despise him because he did not beat her. And in the village, too, there was no one who cared about the youth. Mariana, the cossack's daughter, had laughed at him when he declared that he wanted to marry her, and after that Alyosha had not asked any of the other girls to accept him as their groom. No one wanted to bring him into the Zaporozhian Sich,* because he looked too weakly and perhaps was also a bit too young.

He had already run away to the nearest monastery once, but the monks would not take him in. And so there was nothing left for him but the steppe, the wide-open, rolling steppe. A hunter had once given him an old rifle; God alone knows what it used for ammunition. Alyosha always carried it with him, but he never shot it, first of all because he wanted to save the charge, and then because he did not know why he should.

One mild, quiet evening at the beginning of the summer, everyone was sitting together at the crude table, on which was a bowl of kasha. Peter ate, and the others watched him, waiting for his leavings. Suddenly, the old man stopped with his spoon poised in the air and extended his broad, wizened head into the shaft of light that came through the door and crossed the table into the shadows. Everyone listened. Outside there was a noise on the walls of the hut, a sound like that of a night bird brushing its wings against the beams. But the sun

*The Zaporozhian Sich, or armed camp, was the stronghold of the Cossacks in Zaporozhia.—Ed.

had barely set, and on top of that the birds of the night rarely came into the village. And there it was again—as though some large animal were groping around the house and as though its searching steps could be heard from all the walls at once. Alyosha rose stealthily from the bench, and at the same moment something darkened the door, something tall and black. It completely eclipsed the evening light, bringing night into the hut, and for all its size moved forward only with uncertainty.

"It's Ostap!" said the ugly girl in her malicious voice. And now everyone recognized him. He was one of the blind *kobzars*, or bards, an old man who with his twelve-string bandura traveled through the villages singing of the great fame of the Cossacks, of their courage and loyalty, of their hetmans* Kirdyaga, Kukubenko, Bulba, and other heroes, songs that all were glad to hear. Ostap made three deep bows in the direction where he thought the image of the saint was (and it was to the Znamenskaya, the Virgin Mother, that he thus inadvertently turned), sat down by the stove, and asked in a soft voice:

"In whose house am I, actually?"

"You're in our house, little father, the house of Peter Akimovitch, the shoemaker," replied Peter with kindness. He was a lover of songs, and this unexpected visit made him happy.

"Oh, at the house of Peter Akimovitch, the painter of pictures," said the blind man, by way of returning the kindness. Then he fell silent. A sound arose from the six long strings of the bandura. It swelled and then came

*A hetman is a Cossack chief.—Ed.

back from the six short strings, foreshortened and as though exhausted. And this effect was repeated in ever-faster cadences, until the point was reached where the listeners had to close their eyes for fear they might see the sounds of the furiously mounting melody crashing to earth somewhere. Then the song of the strings ended and made room for the beautiful, full voice of the *kobzar*, which soon filled the whole house and went beyond it to call forth the people from the neighboring huts, who gathered in front of the door and beneath the windows. But the song was not about the heroes this time. The fame of Bulba and Ostranitza and Naliwaiko was already secure. Established for all time was the loyalty of the Cossacks. The song was not about their deeds. And more deeply asleep still, as it seemed to the listeners, was dance; for no one stirred a foot or raised a hand. Like Ostap's own, the heads of all were bowed low, made heavy by the sadness of the song.

"There is no justice left in the world. Justice, who can find it? There is no justice left in the world; for all justice is bound by the laws of injustice.

"Today, Justice lies in chains, agonizing. And Injustice laughs over her, we have seen it, and sits with the *pans* on golden seats and sits in the golden hall with the *pans.*

"Justice lies at the threshold and begs; the guest within, in the house of the *pans*, is Injustice, the evil one. They invite her with laughter into their palace, and for Injustice they pour the full flagon of mead.

"O Justice, little mother, little mother mine, on your pinions, like those of an eagle, another may come, a just man, one who will be just. Then God help him, who alone can, to lighten the days of the just."

And heads were lifted, only with effort, and on all countenances could be read a reluctance to speak, which was seen also by those who wanted to speak. And after a short, grave silence, the music of the bandura resumed, this time better understood by the steadily growing crowd. Three times Ostap sang his song of justice. And each time it was a different song. If the first time it had been a lament, when it was repeated it seemed to be an accusation; and finally, when the *kobzar* shouted it out for the third time like a series of short commands with his head raised high, a savage wrath broke forth from the quivering words and took hold of all present and set them off into a vast, but at the same time anxious, frenzy.

"Where are the men gathering?" asked a young peasant as the singer was rising from his place. The old man, who was well informed about all the movements of the Cossacks, named a nearby place. The men scattered quickly. Brief outcries could be heard, weapons were taken up, and in front of their doorways, the women cried. An hour later, a company of armed peasants set forth from the town in the direction of Chernigov.

Peter had offered the *kobzar* a glass of cider in the hope of finding out more from him. The old man sat there, drank, but provided only curt answers to the shoemaker's many questions. Then he said his thanks and departed. Alyosha led the blind man over the threshold. When they were outside in the night and alone, Alyosha asked him, "Can anyone join in the war?"

"Anyone," said the old man, and disappeared at a quick pace, as though he could see in the dark.

When everyone was asleep, Alyosha got up off the

stove, where he had been lying with his clothes on, took his rifle, and went out. Outside, all at once he felt himself being embraced and kissed gently on his hair. Immediately, then, in the moonlight he recognized Akulina, who was dashing toward the house.

"Mother?" he called out, surprised, and he began to feel very odd. He hesitated for a time. A door closed somewhere and a dog howled nearby. Then Alyosha hung his rifle over his shoulder and set off vigorously, for he intended to catch up with the men before morning. But in the house, everyone behaved as though they did not notice Alyosha's absence. Only when they resumed their places at the table and Peter noticed the empty place did he get up, go to the corner, and light a candle before the Znamenskaya. A very thin candle. The ugly daughter shrugged her shoulders.

Meanwhile, Ostap, the blind old man, had already arrived at the next village and was beginning, sadly and with a gently plaintive voice, the "Song of Justice."

The crippled man bided his time for a few moments. Then he looked at me with surprise. "So, why don't you tell the end? It must be as in the treachery story—the old man was God."

"Oh," I said with a shudder, "I hadn't realized."

A Scene from the Venice Ghetto

Mr. Baum, house owner, chairman of the district council, honorary chief of the volunteer fire department, and possessor of various other distinctions—but to come to the point, Mr. Baum must have eavesdropped on one of my conversations with Ewald. It's no wonder. He is the owner of the house my friend lives in on the ground floor. Mr. Baum and I—we know each other a long time by sight. The other day, however, the chairman of the district council stopped and raised his hat a bit—just enough for a small bird to fly out in case one had been trapped under it. Smiling politely, he initiated our acquaintance with these words:

"Do you sometimes travel?"

"Oh, yes," I replied, a little absent-mindedly, "that could well be."

Now he continued in a familiar tone, "I think we're the only two around here who have been to Italy."

"Oh," I said, trying to focus a bit more clearly. "Well, yes, in that case it is of course urgently necessary for us to have a conversation."

Mr. Baum laughed. "Yes, Italy, it's really something. I always tell my children—take Venice, for example."

"You still remember Venice?"

"Oh, but please," he groaned, for he was a bit too fat to show indignation without effort, "how could I not? . . . once you've seen it . . . that Piazzetta . . . don't you agree?"

"Yes," I replied. "I especially remember with pleasure those rides through the canals, gliding soundlessly by those remnants of the past."

"The Palazzo Franchetti," he recalled.

"The Cà Doro," I countered.

"The Fish Market—"

"The Palazzo Vendramin—"

"Where Richard Wagner . . ." he hastened to add as an educated German. I nodded.

"The Ponte, you know?"

He smiled with recognition. "Of course, and the museum, and let's not forget the Academy, where a Titian . . ."

In this fashion Mr. Baum subjected himself to a kind of examination, which cost him a fair effort. It occurred to me to compensate him by telling him a story. And I began without further ado.

"When you ride under the Ponte di Rialto past the Fondaco de' Turchi and the Fish Market, and you tell the gondolier, 'To the right!' he looks at you with surprise and might well even ask, '*Dove?*' But you insist on going to the right, and you get out in one of those dirty little canals, bargain with him, tell him off, and walk away through crowded back streets and passages filled with black smoke toward an empty, open square. You do all this simply because that's where my story takes place."

Mr. Baum touched me lightly on the arm. "Excuse me, what story?" His small eyes moved back and forth somewhat nervously.

"Just a story, worthy sir," I calmed him, "nothing particularly remarkable. I also can't tell you when it happened. Maybe under Doge Alvise Mocenigo IV, but it might also have been somewhat earlier or later. The paintings of Carpaccio, in case you might have seen those, seem to have been painted on purple velvet. Something warm, something, as it were, of the forest comes off every part of them, and eavesdropping shadows huddle around the subdued lights within them. Giorgione painted on dull, antiqued gold, and Titian on black satin. But during the time I'm talking about, people liked pictures that were light and bright, done on a ground of white silk. And the name people were bandying about, that sprang from beautiful lips into the sunshine and that charming ears caught when it fell quivering back down—that name was Giovanni Battista Tiepolo."

But none of that appears in my story. That all has to do only with the real Venice, the city of palaces, of adventures, of balls, of pale nights on the lagoons, which carry the sounds of secret romances as no other nights do. But in the part of Venice where my story occurs, there are only poor, everyday noises. The days pass over it, each like the day before, as though there were only one, and the songs you hear there are swelling laments that do not rise but lie over the narrow streets like seething fumes. As soon as dusk falls, a shy rabble comes out and goes about its business. Countless children have their homes in the squares and in cold, narrow doorways, where they play with shards of broken pots and with multicolored pieces left over from the glass works, the same material out of which the masters put together the solemn mosaics of San Marco. An aristocrat seldom finds his way into the Ghetto. The most likely time is when the Jewish girls come to the well; perhaps at that time one might see a figure in a black cloak wearing a mask. Certain people know from experience that this figure carries a dagger hidden in the folds of his cloak. Someone claims to have seen the face of the youth, and since that time it has been said that the slender, black-clad guest is Marcantonio Priuli, the son of Proveditore Nicolo Priuli and the beautiful Catharina Minelli. People know that he waits under the portico of Isaac Rosso's house; then, when the square empties of people, he crosses it and goes into the house of old Melchizedek, the rich goldsmith, who has many sons and seven daughters and from those sons and daughters, many grandchildren.

The youngest of his granddaughters, Esther, is expecting him and waits close at the side of her aged grandfather in a low, dark chamber in which much glitters and glows, and silk and velvet hang softly over the coffers as though to dampen their full, golden flames. Here sits Marcantonio on a silver-embroidered cushion at the foot of the elderly Jew and tells him of Venice as though recounting a fairy tale that never came true so completely anywhere else. He tells of the plays in the theaters, of the battles of the Venetian armies, of foreign visitors, of paintings and sculptures, of the Festa della Sensa on Ascension Day, of the Carnival, and of the beauty of his mother, Catharina Minelli. All of this has the same meaning for him—these are different expressions of power and love and life. To his two listeners, all of it is foreign, for the Jews are strictly excluded from all such intercourse, and even rich Melchizedek has never entered the jurisdictional sphere of the Great Council, although as a goldsmith and because of the high esteem he enjoyed in general, he might have dared to do so. In the course of his long life, the old man has obtained many privileges from the Council for his coreligionists, all of whom look upon him as a father. But ever and again he has had to suffer the backlash. For whenever a misfortune fell upon the state, revenge for it was taken upon the Jews. The Venetians were far too close to them in the set of their minds ever to have used the Jews, as other peoples have, to accomplish their commerce. Instead they tormented them with taxes, despoiled them of their goods, and reduced the area of the Ghetto ever further, so that its families, who in the face of all their hardship still were fruitful and multiplied, were forced to build their houses in the vertical dimension, one on the roof of another. And their city, which did not lie on the sea, grew slowly into the space of heaven as though it were another sea; and all around the square where the well was, buildings rose in dizzy perpendicularity like the walls of some giant's tower.

Rich Melchizedek, in the eccentricity of advanced age, had made a strange proposal to his fellow citizens and his sons and grandsons. He wished to live in whichever of these tiny houses, jammed in countless stories one on top of the other, was the highest at any given time. People were only too glad to grant him this bizarre wish, since in any case no one any longer trusted the strength of the lower walls, and they built on top of them with such flimsy stones that the wind no longer seemed to take notice of the walls. Thus the old man moved from house to house two or three times a year, and Esther, who was unwilling to abandon him, was always with him. Finally, they were living at such a height that when they stepped out of the narrow confines of their apartment onto the flat roof, their heads already reached a level where a new country began, of whose customs the old man spoke in dark words, as though half caught up in the raptures of a psalm.

It was now a long way up to where they lived, a way that passed through the lives of many unknown people, over steep and slippery steps, past scolding women, past the raiding of hungry children, and the many obstacles with which it was beset stood in the way of any intercourse. Even Marcantonio no longer came to visit, and Esther hardly missed him. She had looked upon him so fully and so long over the hours she had been alone with him that it seemed to her that he had tumbled into the depths of her dark eyes and perished there and was now beginning within her a new and eternal life, the one in which he, as a Christian, had believed. With this new sensation in her young body, she stood through many long days on the roof and searched for the sea. But as high as the building stood, the furthest things that could be made out were the gable of the Palazzo Foscari, some tower or other, the dome of a church—as though frozen in the light—and then a complex pattern of masts, beams, and poles across the edge of the wet, quivering sky.

Toward the end of that summer, in spite of anything anyone could say, and though the climbing was already a hardship for him, the old man moved again. For a new hovel had been built, high above all the rest. And as he was once more walking across the square after so long a time, leaning on Esther's arm, many people crowded around him and bowed low to touch his groping hands and plead for his advice about many things. For he seemed to them like a dead man who had risen from his grave because some prophesied time had at length come to pass. And so it really seemed. The men told him that an uprising was in progress in Venice, that the nobility stood in peril, and that in a short time the boundaries of the Ghetto would fall and everyone would rejoice in the same freedom. The old man had nothing to say in answer, only nodded as though all of this were long since known to him along with much more besides. He went into the house of Isaak Rosso, on the top of which his new apartment was situated, and climbed a full half day to reach it.

Up there, Esther gave birth to a tender blond child. After she had recuperated, she took it out on the roof in her arms and for the first time set before its wide-open eyes the whole golden sky. It was an autumn morning of indescribable clarity and light. Things, objects, were darkened, almost without illumination; only isolated bits of flying light settled on them, as on big flowers, rested there for a moment, and then darted beyond their gold-limned edges into the heavens. And there, where they vanished, from this high vantage point could be seen what had never yet been seen from the Ghetto, a still, silvery light—the sea. And only now, after her eyes had accustomed themselves to this glory, did she make out Melchizedek, over on the edge of the roof, as far forward as one could go. He stood with his arms outspread and forced his dull eyes to look into the slowly unfolding light. His arms remained raised, a radiant thought upon his countenance, as though he were at worship. Then he rocked forward again and again, pressing his old head against the badly cut, sharp-edged stones. People had gathered on the square below and were looking up at him. Individual words and gestures rose up out of the crowd but did not reach the solitary old man in prayer. And the people saw the eldest and the youngest as though in the clouds. But the old man continued for a long while to lift himself up in pride and then fall back again in humility. And the crowd grew, and their eyes did not stir from him. Was it the sea he had seen or God, the Eternal, in His Glory?

Mr. Baum made an effort to come up with a quick response. He did not immediately succeed. "Probably the sea," he said at last, and then added dryly, "it does, after all, make quite an impression," thereby showing himself to be particularly enlightened, a person in the know.

I quickly took my leave, but could not resist calling after him, "Don't forget to recount this to your children."

He thought about this. "To my children? You know, this young nobleman Antonio, or whatever his name was, is a rather unsavory character. And then, the child, this child! We shouldn't really . . . for children—"

"Oh, dear sir," I soothed him, "you've forgotten that children come from God! Why should the children have any doubts about Esther having one, since she lived so close to heaven?"

The children ended up hearing this story too. And when you ask them what they think about what the old Jew Melchizedek might have seen in his rapture, they reply without a moment's thought, "Oh, the sea, too!"

The Man Who Listened to Stones

Once again I am at the house of my crippled friend. He smiles in his own special way and says, "But you never told me any stories about Italy."

"I suppose that means I ought to make up for that as soon as possible?" Ewald nodded and at once closed his eyes to listen. So I began.

What we experience as spring, God sees as a fleeting little smile passing over the earth. The Earth seems to be remembering something, which then in the summer she tells to everyone; until at last she becomes wiser in the great stillness of autumn, which is how she confides in the lonely. All the springs that you and I have lived through, taken all together, do not add up to one of God's seconds. A spring that is to be noticed by God cannot be confined only to the trees and fields; its power must also enter into human beings. For then it continues to happen, not in time, but rather in eternity, so to speak, and in the presence of God.

Once upon a time, when this was happening, God's gaze, in its dark movement back and forth, had to halt over Italy. The land beneath was bright, the time shone like gold; but across this, like a dark road, lay the shadow of a robust man, heavy and black, and far in front of it, the shadow of his hands at work, unquiet, moving spasmodically now over Pisa, now over Naples, now melting into the uncertain motion of the sea. God could not take His eyes off these hands, which first appeared to Him to be joined as in prayer—but the prayer that welled up from them was driving them far apart. There was a silence in the heavens. All the saints followed God's gaze and contemplated, as He was doing, the shadows that veiled half of Italy, and the hymns of angels froze on their faces, and the stars trembled, for they were afraid they had been guilty of some fault, and they waited humbly for God's word of wrath. But nothing of the sort came to pass. The heavens had opened in their full breadth over Italy, so that Raphael was on his knees in Rome, and the holy Fra Angelico of Fiesole stood in a cloud and rejoiced over him. At this time, many prayers were on their way up from the earth. But God took heed of only one; the force of Michelangelo rose up to Him like a fragrance from the vineyards. And He allowed it to fill His thoughts. He leaned lower, found the man at work, looked over his shoulders on down to the hands lying attentively on stone, and was startled: Might there be souls in stones too? Why was this man listening to the stones? And now the hands awakened and pulled on the stone as though digging up a grave in which a weak, dying voice is quavering.

"Michelangelo," God called out anxiously, "who is in the stone?" Then he answered in a dull voice, "You, O Lord, who else? But I can't get at You."

And then God felt that He was in the stone too, and He became afraid and felt closed in. The whole of heaven was a stone, and He was shut up in the middle of it, relying on Michelangelo's hands to liberate Him; and He heard them coming, though still at a distance.

But the master was again at his work. He kept thinking: You are nothing but a small block, and nobody else could find a human being in you. But I feel a shoulder here—it is the shoulder of Joseph of Arimathea; and here Mary bends, I feel her trembling hands, holding Jesus, our Lord, who has just died on the Cross. If there is room for these three in this small piece of marble, why should I not be able to draw out of a large rock a whole sleeping race? And with broad strokes he freed from the marble the three figures of the *Pietà*, but he did not entirely take away the stony veil from their faces, as though he feared their deep grief might fall upon his hands and lame them. And so he fled to another piece of stone. But in each piece of work he lacked the courage to give a brow its full clarity or a shoulder it purest roundness, and if he was forming a woman, he stopped shy of putting the final smile on her lips so as not to expose her full beauty.

At this time, he was designing the monument for Julius della Rovere's tomb. His idea was to build a mountain over the Iron Pope and create a race to people that mountain. Filled with many obscure plans, he went out to his marble quarry. Its steep slope rose above a poor village. Amid the olive trees and old faded rock, the freshly split surfaces looked like a large pale face under an old man's hair. Michelangelo stood for a long time in front of its veiled brow. Suddenly he saw beneath it two gigantic eyes of stone, which were looking at him. And Michelangelo felt his form grow under the influence of that gaze. Now he too towered above the landscape, and it seemed to him that he had stood facing this mountain like a brother for all eternity. The valley fell away below him as below a climber, the huts crowded together like cattle, and the face in the rock looked nearer and easier to relate to under its white stony veils. It had a waiting expression, motionless yet on the verge of movement. Michelangelo reflected: "You cannot be broken into pieces, since you are but one." And then he raised his voice, "I will complete you; you are my work." And he turned back toward Florence. He saw a star and the tower of the cathedral. And it was evening around his feet.

All at once, at the Porta Romana, he hesitated. The two rows of houses stretched toward him like arms, and all at once they took hold of him and pulled him into the city. And the city lanes became ever narrower and murkier, and as he entered his house, he knew himself to be in dark hands from which he could not escape. He fled into the main room and from there into the low chamber, hardly two paces long, where he was in the habit of writing. Its walls pressed in on him, and it was as though they were fighting against his disproportionate size and squeezing him back down into his old, limited form. And he allowed it. He forced himself to his knees and let them shape him. He felt within himself a humility he had never known and even had the wish somehow to become small. And a voice came:

"Michelangelo, who is in you?"

And the man in the confined chamber laid his head heavily in his hands and said softly, "You, O Lord, who else?"

And then things broadened out around God, and He lifted His face, which was over Italy, freely upward and looked around Him: in their cloaks and miters, the saints were standing there and the angels were going about among the thirsting stars with their songs like vessels full of glistening spring water, and to heaven there was no end.

My crippled friend raised his gaze and allowed the evening clouds to draw it with them across the sky. "Is God there, then?" he asked.

I made no answer. Then I leaned over to him and said, "Ewald, are we here, then?" And we held each other warmly by the hand.

How the Thimble Came to Be the Dear Lord

As I stepped back from the window, the evening clouds were stilled there. They seemed to be waiting. Ought I to tell them a story too? I made the suggestion to them. But they did not hear me at all. In order to make myself understood and to reduce the distance between us, I called out:

"I am an evening cloud too." They paused in their movement; obviously they were observing me. Then they extended their fine, translucent reddish wings toward me. That is the way that evening clouds greet one another. They had recognized me.

"We are over the earth," they explained, "to be more exact, over Europe. And you?" I hesitated. "There's a country there. . . ."

"What does it look like?" they inquired.

"Well," I replied, "twilight with things in it."

"That's the same with Europe too," laughed a young cloud.

"Possibly," I said, "but I have always heard that the things in Europe are dead."

"Yes, of course," another one remarked scornfully. "What kind of nonsense is that—things that are alive?"

"Well," I insisted, "mine are alive. So that's the difference. They can become various other things, and just because an object comes into the world as a pencil or a stove, it does not have to despair of getting beyond that. A pencil might become a stick or, if all goes well, a mast, a stove, or at least a city gate."

"You seem quite a simple-minded evening cloud to me," said the young cloud that had expressed itself in such an unrestrained manner earlier on. An elder cloud, fearing that it might have offended me, tried to smooth things over:

"There are all kinds of countries, very different from one another. I once found myself over a small German principality, and to this day I still don't believe it was part of Europe."

I thanked him and said, "I see that we're not going to have an easy time agreeing on this. With your permission, I'll simply tell you what I have been seeing beneath me recently. That will be the best solution."

"Please be so kind," the elder courteously allowed on behalf of all present. So I began.

> There are people in a room. I am rather high, you must know, and as a result of this they look like children to me. For that reason, I would prefer simply to say "children." So then, there are some children in a room. Two, five,

six, seven children. It would take too long to ask them their names. Moreover, it seems the children are in the midst of an animated discussion; and in the course of that, one or another of them will name names anyhow. They must already have been at it for some time, for the oldest of them (I hear them calling him Hans) is remarking as though by way of conclusion:

"No, it definitely can't go on like that. I've heard that in the old days every evening—or at least on evenings when they'd been good—the parents told the children stories until they fell asleep. Does anything like that go on these days?" After a short pause, Hans answers himself. "It doesn't happen—anywhere. For my part, and also since I'm already something of a grownup, I would be happy to make them a gift of those few miserable dragons that they trouble themselves over so; but all the same, it is only fitting that they should tell us there are such things as nixies, dwarves, princes, and monsters."

"I have an aunt," says a little girl, "who sometimes tells me—"

"Hey, there," Hans cut her off short, "aunts don't count. They're liars." The whole group was quite taken aback by this bold assertion, which nevertheless remained unrefuted. Hans continues. "Also, what we're mainly talking about here is the parents, because they're the ones who are more or less obligated to instruct us in these matters. For the others, it's more an act of kindness. They can't be required to do it. But see here, what do our parents do? They walk around with long, troubled faces, nothing suits them, they shout and scold, but at the same time they're so apathetic they would hardly notice it if the world came to an end. They have these things they call 'ideals.' Maybe those are another kind of little children that can't be left alone and that are also a drain on their strength—but then they shouldn't have had us!

"Well, children, the way I see it is this: the fact that our parents neglect us is sad, for sure. But we would put up with that anyhow if it were not a proof that grownups in general are getting stupid. They are regressing, if I may put it that way. We cannot put a stop to their decline, since we have no influence on them the whole day; and when we come home late from school, no one could ask us at that point to sit down with them and try to get them interested in something reasonable. And what a pain it is to sit for hours under the study lamp and have a mother who still doesn't even understand the Pythagorean theorem! Well, that's the way it is. And so the grownups will keep getting dumber. . . . But what harm does it do, what do we lose by it? Breeding? They take their hats off to each other, but if a bald head is revealed in the process, they laugh. On the whole, they laugh constantly. If we did not have the good sense to cry now and then, there would be no balance in these things either. But at the same time they are so arrogant, they even assert that the kaiser is a grownup. I've read in the papers that the king of Spain is a child, and the same is true of all kings and kaisers, don't let anyone try to tell you otherwise! But along with all the things that don't matter, the grownups do have something we can't afford to be indifferent to—God, the dear Lord. It's true that I have yet to see Him at any of their houses, and that by itself is suspicious. It has even occurred to me that maybe, in the midst of their distraction, constant activity, and rushing about, they might have lost Him somewhere. But He is definitely something we can't do without. There are various things that can't happen without Him. The sun can't rise, children can't be born, and also there'd be an end to bread. Even though it comes out at the baker's, it's the dear Lord who turns the big millstones. Many reasons can easily be found why the dear Lord is something indispensable. But this much is sure: the grownups don't look after Him, so we children have to do it. Listen to the plan I've worked out. There are exactly seven of us children. Each one of us must carry God with us for one day; then He will be with us the whole week, and we'll always know where He is at a given moment."

Here an awkward problem emerged. How could this be done? Was it possible to pick up God in one's hands or stick Him in one's pocket? In this connection, one of the little ones recounted: "I was alone in my room. A little lamp was burning near me, and I was sitting in bed saying my evening prayer—very loudly. Something moved in my joined hands. It was soft and warm like a little bird. I couldn't open my hands, because the prayer wasn't over yet. But I was very curious and prayed terribly fast. Then when I got to 'amen' I went like this"—the little boy stretched out his hands and spread his fingers—"but there was nothing there."

This they could all imagine. And even Hans didn't know what to do. Everybody looked at him. And all at once he said, "This is really dumb. Anything could be God. You just have to tell it." He turned to a red-haired boy standing next to him. "It can't be an animal. It would run away. But a thing, you see, will stand still. You come into the room day or night, and it's always there. That could be God." Little by little the others were convinced. "But we need a small object that you can carry around everywhere with you. Otherwise the whole thing doesn't make sense. So empty all your pockets."

Only very odd things appeared: scraps of paper, penknives, erasers, feathers, lengths of string, small stones, screws, whistles, wood shavings, and much else that couldn't be recognized at a distance or that I don't have a name for. And all these things lay in the children's shallow palms as though terrified at the sudden possibility of becoming God, but those among them that were able to shine a little bit shone, so that they might find favor with Hans. The choice hung in the balance for a long time. Finally, in little Resi's possession was found a thimble, which she had once taken from her mother. It was bright as though made from silver, and because of its beauty, it became God. Hans himself took it, for he was the first in line, and the whole day the children followed him around and were proud of him. It was not easy to agree who would have it the next day, so Hans judiciously then and there set up the schedule for the whole week, so that there would be no disputes.

On the whole, this arrangement proved to be quite practical. It could be seen at first glance who had God at any moment, for the child in question walked in a somewhat more stiff and formal fashion and had the kind of expression on his or her face hitherto reserved for Sundays. The first three days the children spoke of nothing else. At every moment one of them was asking to see

God, and though the thimble had not changed at all under the influence of its great prestige, the thimbleness of it now seemed to be only a humble covering over its true form.

Everything proceeded according to plan. On Wednesday, Paul had it, on Thursday, little Anna. Saturday came. The children were playing catch and tumbling about breathlessly when Hans suddenly cried, "Who has God?" Everybody stood up. Everyone looked at everyone else. Nobody remembered seeing Him for two days. Hans counted out whose turn it was, and it came out to be little Mary. And then everyone unceremoniously demanded God from little Mary. What to do? The little girl scratched around in her pockets. Now at last she remembered that she had received Him in the morning; but now He was gone. Probably she had lost Him here while playing.

And when the children went home, the little girl remained behind in the meadow and kept looking. The grass was rather high. Twice people came by and asked what she had lost. Each time the child answered, "A thimble," and continued her search. The people helped her look for a while, but soon got tired of bending over, and one of them called to her as he was leaving, "You're better off going home, you can buy a new one." But little Mary kept on looking.

The meadow became more and more alien as the dusk fell, and the grass began to get wet. Then another man came. He bent over the child and asked, "What are you looking for?" Now little Mary, who was not far from tears, answered bravely and defiantly, "The dear Lord."

The stranger smiled and simply took her by the hand, and she let herself be led along as though everything were now fine. As they were walking along, the strange man said, "Now look what a pretty thimble I found today."

The evening clouds had long since become impatient. Now the wise elder cloud, who had become fat in the meantime, turned to me and said:

"Excuse me, but may I not hear the name of the country over which you—" but the other clouds ran off laughing into the sky and dragged the old man cloud after them.

A Tale of Death with a Strange Postscript

I was still staring up into the gradually dimming evening sky when somebody said, "You seem to be very interested in that land up there."

My gaze fell fast, as though shot down, and I saw that I had arrived in my walk at the low wall of our little churchyard and that in front of me, on the other side of it, stood a man with a shovel in his hand and a serious smile on his face.

"Whereas I'm interested in this land down here," he finished up, pointing at the damp, black earth that peeked through in many spots from beneath the withered leaves that were stirring noisily—while I hadn't even realized a wind had come up.

Suddenly, seized by a powerful revulsion, I said, "Why are you doing that?"

The gravedigger continued to smile. "It's a living," he said, "and then too, most people do the same as I do, don't you agree? They bury God up there the way I do people here." He pointed up at the sky and explained to me, "That's a big grave too. In the summer wild forget-me-nots grow on it—"

"There was a time," I interrupted him, "when people buried God in heaven, that's true."

"Has that changed?" he asked with a strange sadness.

"At one time," I continued, "everyone did throw a handful of heaven over Him, I know that. But at that point He actually wasn't there anymore, or maybe He was . . ." I hesitated.

"You know," I started up again, "in olden times, people used to pray like this." I spread my arms out and felt my chest involuntarily expand.

> At that time, God was casting Himself into all those abysses full of humility and darkness, and He would return only reluctantly to heaven, which, unnoticed, He was pulling down ever closer over the earth. But a new faith sprang up. And since this faith was unable to make people understand how its new God was different from the old one (since as soon as it began to praise Him, the people immediately recognized one and the same old God in this one too), the proclaimer of this new order changed the way of praying. He taught people how to join their hands and ruled as follows: "See, our God wants to be prayed to like this, so therefore He is different from the one that until now you believed you were receiving in your embrace." The people accepted this,

and the gesture of opening the arms came to be looked on with contempt and horror, and later it was fastened to the Cross to show it to everyone as a symbol of misery and death.

But the next time God looked down upon the earth, He recoiled with fear. Next to the multitude of joined hands, people had built many Gothic churches, with the result that the hands and the roofs, equally steep and sharp, were pointing up at Him like hostile weapons. God has a different kind of courage. He turned back into His heaven, and when He noticed that the towers and the new prayers were multiplying behind His back, He departed from His heaven by going out the other side, thus withdrawing Himself from the persecution. He Himself was surprised to find on the other side of His radiant dwelling place an incipient darkness that received Him in silence; and with a strange feeling He went ever further into this obscurity, which reminded Him of the hearts of human beings. At that point it occurred to Him for the first time that while the heads of human beings are brightly lit, their hearts are full of a similar darkness, and He was overcome by a longing to dwell in the hearts of human beings and not to have to go into the clear, cold wakefulness of their thoughts anymore. Well, God has continued on His way. The darkness around Him grows ever thicker, and the night through which He is pushing His way has something of the fragrant warmth of fertile clods of earth. And before too long, roots will reach out toward Him with the beautiful old gesture of open prayer. There is nothing wiser than the circle. The God who fled from us into the heavens will come to us again out of the earth. And, who knows, maybe you are the very person who one day will dig open the gate.

"But that's only a fairy tale," said the man with the shovel.

"In our way of talking," I replied softly, "everything becomes a fairy tale, because for that way of talking it can never have happened."

The man gazed into space for a time. Then, with a gruff gesture, he pulled on his coat and asked, "We can walk together, can't we?"

I nodded. "I'm going home. I suppose it's on your way. But don't you live here?"

He came out of the little fence gate and closed it gently on its wailing hinges. "No," he replied.

After a few paces, he was readier to confide in me. "You were entirely right before. It is strange that you can't find anyone who likes doing that work out there. I never used to think about it. But now that I'm getting older, sometimes I have thoughts, odd thoughts, like that one about heaven, and others too. Death. What do we know about it? Seemingly everything and perhaps nothing. Often when I'm working, the children (I don't know whose they are) hang around me. And just at that time I might have one of those thoughts. Then I dig like an animal in order to draw all the force out of my head and use it up with my arms. The grave gets much deeper than the ordinance requires, and a mountain of earth builds up next to it. But the children see my wild movements and run away. They somehow think I'm angry." He stopped to ponder. "And it is a kind of anger. You lose your sensitivity to it, you think you've got it beat, and suddenly . . . There's no help for it; death is something incomprehensible. Awful."

We were walking in a long street under fruit trees that were already entirely without leaves, and the woods started up on our left like a night that might fall upon us at any time. "I'd like to recount a story to you," I said tentatively. "It will take us just about to where we're going." The man nodded and lit up his little old pipe. I began the story.

There were two people, a man and woman, and they loved each other. Loving—that means assuming nothing, bringing nothing along from anywhere else, forgetting everything, and being ready to receive from one person what you had before and everything else besides. And this was the mutual wish of both of these people. But in time, in the daylight, among the many, all the things that come and go, often before you can develop a relationship to them, do not let this kind of loving take place. Events come at you from all sides, and chance opens every door for them.

For this reason, the two people decided to leave time and go into solitude, far away from the striking of clocks and the noises of the city. And there, in a garden, they built a house. And the house had two entrances, one on its right side and one on its left. The right entrance was the man's entrance, and everything belonging to him was supposed to come into the house through that. But the left entrance was the woman's, and what related to her was supposed to enter that way. And so it happened. The first one to get up in the morning went downstairs and opened his or her door. And until late in the night, much came in that way, even though the house was not right on the side of the road.

For those who know how to receive, the landscape enters the house, as well as the light and a wind with fragrant shoulders, and much more besides. But also things from the past, figures, destinies, came in through both entrances, and they all enjoyed the same simple hospitality, with the result that they felt that they had dwelled from all time in the house on the meadow.

And thus it went on for a long time, and the two people were very happy. The left entrance was opened somewhat more often than the other, but through the right, more colorful guests came in. Before that door one morning, Death was also waiting. The man hurriedly closed his door when he saw him, and the whole day through held it tightly shut. After a time, Death appeared before the left entrance. Trembling, the woman slammed the door and shoved home the heavy bolt. They did not speak with each other about this occurrence, but they opened the two entrances more rarely and tried to make do with what they had in the house. Now, of course, they lived in much greater poverty than they had before. Their supplies grew scant, and they were troubled. They both began to sleep badly, and during one of their long sleepless nights, suddenly they both heard at the same time a strange shuffling and rattling noise. It was behind the wall of the house, equally far from both entrances, and it sounded as though someone were starting to break out stones to make a new entrance in the middle of the wall. The two people, however, behaved in their terror as though they'd heard nothing special. They began to talk, they laughed unnaturally loud, and when they were tired out, the digging sound in the wall died away. Since that time, both entrances have remained completely shut up. The people live like prisoners. Both have become sickly and have strange fantasies. The noise is repeated from time to time. Then they laugh with their lips, while their hearts nearly die from fear. And they both know that the digging has become louder and clearer, and they have to talk and laugh ever louder with their ever-feebler voices.

I fell silent. "Yes, yes," said the man beside me, "that's the way it is; it's a true story."

"I read this one in an old book," I added, "and a very curious thing happened. Next to the line that told how Death appeared in front of the woman's entrance too, a small star was drawn, in old faded ink. It shone out from among the words as from behind a cloud, and for a moment I thought that if the lines were spread apart, it might be revealed that behind them was a sky full of stars, just the way it sometimes happens when the spring sky clears late in the evening. Then I completely forgot this trivial incident, until I found the same little star in the inside back cover of the book, as though reflected in a lake on the smooth glossy paper; and just below it began tender lines that ran like waves over the pale shiny surface. The writing had become indistinct in a number of places, but I was able to decipher it almost completely. This is more or less what was written there":

I have read this story so often, and indeed on all possible kinds of days, that I sometimes think I wrote it myself from memory. But for me, it continues on as I now write. The woman had never seen Death. She let him in without suspecting anything. But Death hurriedly said, like someone who does not have a clear conscience, "Give this to your husband." And when the woman looked at him questioningly, he hastily added, "It's seed, very good seed." Then he departed, without looking back.

The woman opened the little bag that he had put in her hand. There were in truth some kind of seeds inside—hard, ugly kernels. Then the woman thought: a seed is something unfinished, something for the future. There's no way of knowing what will sprout from it. I won't give these nasty kernels to my husband; they don't look at all like a gift. Instead, I'll plant them in the flowerbed in our garden and wait and see what comes up. Then I'll take him there, and tell him how this plant came to me. And that's what the woman did.

Then they continued on with their life in the same way as before. The man, who was continually troubled by the thought of how Death had stood at his door, was somewhat fearful at the beginning, but seeing his wife as welcoming and carefree as ever, he too soon opened the wide wings of his entrance, with the result that lots of light and life came into the house. The next spring, in the middle of the flowerbed, among the slender tiger lilies, there appeared a small shrub. It had narrow, blackish leaves, somewhat pointed, similar to those of the laurel, and there was a weird shine on their dark surface. Every day the man intended to ask where this plant had come from, but every day he let it pass. With a feeling akin to his, from one day to the next, the woman neglected to supply the explanation. But the suppressed question on the one side and the never-dared answer on the other often brought the two people together before this shrub that in its green darkness differed in such a strange way from the rest of the garden.

When the next spring came, they cared for this shrub too, along with the other things in the garden; and they were sad when, though surrounded by flourishing blossoms, it came unchanged and mute, just as in the first year, impervious to all the sunshine. At that time they decided, without letting each other know about it, to devote all their energy the third spring to just this plant. And when that spring came, gently and hand in hand, they fulfilled the promise each had made. The surrounding garden grew wild, and the tiger lilies were paler than usual. But one morning, when they came into the still, glistening garden after a heavy, overcast night, they already knew. From among the black, sharp leaves of the strange shrub had grown a flawless pale blue blossom, for which the bud casing on all sides had already become too small. And they stood before it, united and unspeaking, and now they really did not know what to say to each other. For they were thinking: Death is blossoming now. And they bent down to savor the fragrance of the young bloom. But since that morning, everything in the world has changed.

"That's what it said in the inside cover of the old book," I concluded.

"And who wrote it?" the man urged.

"A woman, judging by the writing," I replied. "But what good would it have done to try to find out? The characters were already very faded and somewhat old-fashioned. Probably she was long since dead."

The man was absorbed in his thoughts. "It's only a story," he admitted at last, "but it touches a person so."

"Well, that's the way it is, when one rarely hears stories," I soothed him.

"You think so?" he said. He extended his hand, and I held it tight. "But I'd like to tell it to someone else. May I do that?" I nodded. Suddenly something occurred to him. "But I have nobody. Who would I tell it to?"

"Oh, that's simple—to the children who sometimes come to watch you. Who else?"

And the children have indeed come to hear the last three stories. Although, if I have been correctly informed, they only got part of the one that the evening clouds retold. The children are after all small, and thus a lot farther from the evening clouds than we are. But with this story, that's fine. For in spite of the long, eloquent speech by Hans, they would see that the thing had taken place among children and, as experts, would take a critical view of the way I told the story. And it is better for them not to find out how hard it is for us to go through things that come to them so effortlessly and simply—and how awkwardly we do it.

An Association That Arose Out of a Crying Need

I have just learned that our little town possesses a kind of artists' association. It recently came into existence, as you can easily imagine, out of a crying need, and people say it is "flourishing." When associations haven't the faintest idea what they should be doing, that is when they flourish. They must have heard that this is the right approach to take in order to be a proper association.

I don't have to tell you that Mr. Baum is an honorary member of the association, its founder, its honorary standard bearer, and everything else all rolled into one; and he has trouble keeping all these roles separate. He sent a young man to invite me to participate in the association's "evenings." I thanked him, it goes without saying, very politely, but added that the whole of my activity over the last five years has consisted in doing just the opposite. "Just imagine," I explained to him with the appropriate gravity, "that not a minute has passed during this period of time when I have not been walking out on some club or association. And yet there still remain societies that, so to speak, contain me."

The young man looked down at my feet, at first with shock and then with an expression of respectful sympathy. He must have seen the "walking out" in them, for he nodded his head with understanding. This result suited me fine, and since just at that moment I had to go out, I proposed that he accompany me part of the way. So we walked through the town and then beyond it toward the train station, for I had errands to take care of in the outlying area. We talked about a variety of things. I learned that the young man was a musician. He had informed me of this with humility; you couldn't tell it by the look of him. Apart from the abundance of his hair, he was distinguished by a great, as it were, leaping eagerness to be of service. Along our not terribly long way together, he picked up my glove twice, held my umbrella as I was looking for something in my pocket, blushingly called my attention to the fact that I had something caught in my beard, that I had a soot spot on my nose—and at this point his thin fingers lengthened, as though craving to get near my face to help me out in this connection. In his eagerness, the young man even fell behind from time to time to disengage, with visible pleasure, dried leaves that had gotten caught in the branches of the bushes as they fluttered down. I realized that these continual interruptions were going to cause me to miss the train (the station was still fairly far away), so I decided to tell my companion a story to encourage him to keep up with me. I immediately began:

I'm familiar with the kind of founding that takes place on the basis of a real need. You'll see what I mean. Not so long ago, three painters came together by chance in an old city. The three painters of course did not talk about art. At least that's the way it seemed. They spent the evening in the back room of an old inn telling each other about their travel adventures and experiences of various kinds. Their stories became ever shorter and more literal, until finally they were left with just a few jokes that they kept tossing back and forth.

To prevent any misunderstanding, I must also say right away that these were real artists, the kind that nature, as it were, intends to be such and not artists by chance. This unfruitful evening in the back room can take nothing away from this; indeed you will soon find out how this evening proceeded.

Other people, ordinary profane beings, came to the inn; the artists felt intruded upon and left. From the moment they stepped out the door, they became different people. They walked in the middle of the street, somewhat separated from each other. It is true that traces of laughter remained on their faces, this odd disordering of the features, but their eyes had already become serious and watchful. Suddenly the one in the middle nudged the one on the right. The latter understood him at once. There before them was a street, a narrow one filled with warm, diaphanous shadows. This ran slightly uphill so that one had a very good perspective on it, and there was something extraordinarily mysterious about it, but at the same time familiar. The three artists let this one moment soak into them. They said nothing, for they knew that this could not be expressed in words. After all, they had become painters because there is much that cannot be spoken. Suddenly the moon rose somewhere, tracing a single gable in silver, and a song was heard rising from a courtyard. "Cheap effects," grumbled the middle one, and they continued walking.

Now they were walking a little closer together, even though they still took up the whole breadth of the street. In this way, they came unexpectedly to a square. Now it was the one on the right who alerted the other two. The moon had done nothing to disrupt this broader, more open scene; on the contrary, it was fairly well necessary for it to be there. It made the square look bigger and imbued the houses with a surprising, listening life; and the lit-up cobbled expanse of the square was rudely interrupted in the middle by a fountain and its heavy shadow, a bold stroke that impressed the painters extraordinarily. They stood closer together and, so to speak, sucked on the breasts of this mood. But they were unpleasantly interrupted. Hurried, light footsteps approached; from the darkness around the fountain emerged a male figure, who received those footsteps and whatever else went with them with the customary tenderness, and all at once the beautiful square was turned into a low-grade illustration, upon which the three painters, acting as but a single painter, turned their back.

"There's that damned novelistic element again," cried the one on the right, using the correct technical term to indicate the pair of lovers by the fountain. United in their resentment, the painters continued to wander the city randomly for a long time, constantly discovering new motifs, but each time offended again by the way in which some banal factor always ruined the stillness and simplicity of every image. By midnight they were back at the inn, in the room of the one on the left, the youngest of them, with no thought as yet of going to sleep. Their nocturnal wandering had awakened a plethora of plans and projects in them, and since they had just had it proved to them that they were of one mind, they now exchanged their respective views with the highest level of interest. No one could say that they produced flawless prose. They threw around a few terms that no ordinary profane individual would have understood, but among themselves they understood each other so well using them that the inhabitants of all the neighboring rooms were unable to get to sleep until nearly four in the morning.

And their long session together had a real, tangible result. Something like an association or club had been formed; that is to say, it was actually already there from the moment that the intentions and goals of the three artists had shown themselves to be so closely linked that it was difficult to tell them apart. The first shared resolve of the "association" was fulfilled immediately. The three artists traveled three hours out into the country and rented a farm together. For the foreseeable future, staying in the city would have made no sense. First of all, what the painters wanted to do out in the country was develop a "style," a certain personal confidence, an eye, a hand, and whatever else all those things are called without which a painter can, it is true, live, but not paint. For the development of all these good qualities, it was hoped that staying together—that is, the "association"—would help, and this especially included the honorary member of the association known as Nature. By nature, the painters understand everything that God Himself created or even might have created under certain circumstances. Fences, houses, wells—all these things are, for the most part, of human origin. But after they have stood in the landscape for a while and have taken on certain properties of the trees and bushes and the other things around them, then it is as though they pass over into the possession of God and thus also become the property of painters. For God and artists have the same riches or the same poverty, depending on the case.

Now, in the nature that surrounded the farm the artists had shared, God certainly did not think He possessed any particular treasure. However, it did not take long for the artists to begin to teach Him better. The area was flat, that could not be denied. But the depth of its shadows and the heights of its lights provided abysses and peaks, between which myriads of middle tones did service for those areas of broad meadow and fertile field that make up the material wealth of mountainous regions. There were but few trees, and almost all of these were of the same kind, from a botanical point of view. However, through the feelings they expressed in the longing of a particular branch or the peaceful reverence of a trunk, they seemed to be so many individual beings; and many a willow became a personality whose character, in its many-sidedness and depth, provided the painters with surprise after surprise. Their enthusiasm was so great, they felt themselves so very much at one with this work, that it is not significant that after half a year had passed, each of the three painters moved into his own house. That was certainly a mere matter of space. But there is something else that must be told at this point.

The painters wanted somehow to celebrate the one-year anniversary of their association, from which so much good had come in such a short time, and each of them secretly decided, as a way of doing this, to paint pictures of the houses of the other two. On the appointed day, the three met, each bringing his paintings with him. It so happened that they talked about their respective houses—their locations, their practical aspects, and so on. They became quite involved in this, with the result that during the discussion, each of them forgot the oil sketches he had brought along and late that night came home with the unopened package. How that could have happened is hard to understand. But in addition, during the period that followed they also did not show each other the paintings. And when one of them visited one of the others (which happened ever more rarely because of a great deal of work), he found on his friend's easel sketches from that first period when they were all living together at the same farm. But one time the one on the right (who now also lived on the right, so we can continue to call him that) discovered at the house of the one I have been calling the youngest, one of those never-shown anniversary pictures. He looked it over reflectively for a while and then said with a laugh:

"Look at that, I wasn't at all aware of that. That's not at all bad the way you've captured my house. A really brilliant caricature. You've really got something there, the way you've exaggerated the color and form and the audacious way you've caught my gable, which really does stand out in that way."

The expression that came over the face of the youngest one was not one of his more becoming looks—on the contrary. He was upset and took himself off to the house of the middle artist, the most measured of the three, hoping he would soothe him. For the youngest one was quick to be intimidated by incidents of this sort and tended to doubt his talent. He did not find the middle one at home, so he rummaged around his studio a bit and soon ran across a picture that he found curiously repellent. It was a house, but one that a real fool must live in. That facade! That could only have been built by someone who had no sense of architecture at all and was applying his miserable painter's ideas to a building. All at once the youngest one pushed away the painting as though it had just burned his fingers. On the left edge of the picture he had read the date of that first anniversary and next to it: "The House of Our Youngest." Naturally he did not wait for the inhabitant of the house to return but returned home in a somewhat bad mood.

Since that time the youngest one and the one on the right became wary of each other. They sought their subject matter in things far away and of course did not consider preparing anything for the second anniversary of their so-helpful association. But the middle one, who suspected nothing, worked all the more enthusiastically at painting a subject that was quite near the house of the one on the right. Something vague kept him from choosing his house itself as the point of departure for his work.

When he brought his finished painting to the one who

lived on the right, the latter behaved in a strangely restrained manner, looking at it only fleetingly while remarking on some incidental matter. Then, after a while, he said, "By the way, I had no idea that you had traveled so far over the last period of time."

"What do you mean, traveled? Far?" The middle one didn't understand a word he was saying.

"Well, this excellent work here," the other responded, "obviously some sort of a Dutch motif."

The measured one in the middle broke out into a laugh. "That's rich. Why, this Dutch motif is located right outside your door." And he would not leave off laughing. But his fellow member of the association was not laughing, not laughing at all. He forced a smile out of himself and opined:

"A good joke."

"But not at all. Just open the door and I'll show you." And the one in the middle moved toward the door himself.

"Stop!" his host commanded him. "And let me tell you once and for all that I have never seen this place and also never will see it, because for my eye it is altogether incapable of existing."

"But—" said the middle one, astonished.

"You're going to insist?" the one on the right continued indignantly. "Fine! I'm leaving—today! You're forcing me to leave, because I don't want to live in this place. You understand?"

And that was the end of their friendship—but not of the association. For to this day it has still not been statutorily dissolved. No one has thought of doing it, and we would be fully justified in saying that it has spread over the entire earth.

"Once again," broke in the eager young man, who had already been continuously flexing his lips, "here we see one of those colossal successes of association life. Without a doubt many outstanding masters have been produced by this intimate bonding."

"Allow me," I said as he unexpectedly dusted my sleeve. "This was really just the introduction to my story, although it is more complicated than the story itself. So . . ."

I said that the club had spread over the entire earth, and this is a fact. Its three members fled from one another with genuine horror. Nowhere could they find peace. Each of them lived in constant fear that one of the others might still come to see a bit of the country he lived in and desecrate it with his depraved representation of it. And when they had already arrived at three opposite points on the earth's rim, to each of them came the inconsolable notion that his sky, the sky he had painstakingly taken possession of through his growing uniqueness and originality, was still within reach of the others. In this moment of crisis, they began, all three at the same time, holding their easels, to walk backward. Had they gone five steps farther, they would have fallen off the edge of the earth into the infinite, and would now be obliged to execute with headlong speed the double orbiting movement around the earth and the sun. But the empathy and attention of God prevented this cruel fate. God saw the danger and at the last moment (what else could He have done?) stepped out into the middle of the sky. The three painters recoiled with fright. Then they planted their easels and set up their palettes. This was an opportunity that could not be missed. The dear Lord does not appear every day and also not to everyone. And of course each of the painters believed that God was posing for him alone. And soon they were becoming more and more absorbed in this interesting work. And every time God wants to go back into heaven, Saint Luke requests Him to remain outside for a while longer so that the three painters can finish their pictures.

"And these gentlemen have doubtless already exhibited and perhaps even sold these paintings?" asked the musician in the gentlest tones.

"What can you be thinking of?" I countered. "They're still working on their God paintings, and surely will continue to do so until their own ends have come. However, should they (and I consider this to be out of the question) come together again while they're still alive and show each other the paintings they have painted of God in the meantime, who knows: perhaps these pictures might be barely distinguishable."

And now we had reached the station. I still had five minutes. I thanked the young man for his companionship and wished him all the best for the new association that he was representing in such an outstanding manner. With his right index finger he wiped away the dust that seemed to be burdening the windowsill of the little waiting room, and was quite lost in his thoughts. I must admit that I was already flattering myself that it was my little stories that had made him so pensive. When, by way of farewell, he pulled a small red thread out of my glove, out of gratitude I gave him the following advice: "You can cut across the fields on the way back; that way is significantly shorter than going by the road."

"Pardon me," said the eager young man with a bow, "in any case I shall go back by the road. At this very moment I'm trying to think of where that was. While you were being kind enough to recount some really important things to me, I thought I saw a scarecrow in the field in an old coat, and one of the sleeves, I think the left one, had gotten hung up on the pole so it couldn't blow in the wind at all. I now somehow feel I have a duty to make my small contribution to the general good of humanity—which also seems to me to be a kind of association in which we each have our bit to do—by restoring to this sleeve its true significance, which is to blow in the wind." The young man then retired with the sweetest of smiles. I, on the other hand, nearly missed my train.

Fragments of this story were sung by the young man at one of the "evenings" of the association. God knows who made up the music for them. Mr. Baum, the honorary standard bearer, imparted these to the children, and the children took a liking to some of the melodies.

The Beggar and the Proud Maiden

It happened that we—the schoolteacher and I—were witness to the following small incident. In our town, at the edge of the woods, from time to time an old beggar stands. He was there again today, poorer, more miserable than ever, and through a pitiable mimicry almost indistinguishable from the decrepit board fence on which he was leaning. But then it happened that a very little girl came running up to him to give him a small coin. There was nothing particularly remarkable about this. The only surprising thing was the way she did it. She made a well-behaved, handsome little curtsy, handed her gift to the old man quickly as though to keep it from being noticed, curtsied again, and was quickly gone. These two little curtsies, however, were fit for an emperor at least.

All this sorely vexed our honorable schoolteacher. He immediately wanted to lunge at the beggar, probably to drive him away from his post at the fence. For as we know, he was on the executive committee of the association for the poor and definitely opposed to begging in the streets. I held him back.

"These people are supported by us, indeed, we could even say, cared for," he said heatedly. "If they go beyond that and beg in the street, then that is simply . . . insolence."

"Esteemed sir," I said, trying to calm him down, "I have to tell you a story."

"Is that so urgent?" he asked with a touch of venom. I took him seriously.

"Right here and now. Before you forget what we just had the opportunity to observe." The teacher had been suspicious of me since my last story. I read that on his face and reassured him, "Not about God, really not. The dear Lord does not appear in my story. It's something historical." With that, I won my case. One only has to say the word *history*, and immediately any teacher will prick up his ears. For history is something highly respectable, harmless, and often applicable pedagogically. I noted that our worthy schoolteacher was once again cleaning his spectacles, a sign that his power of vision had passed over into his ears. And I skillfully took advantage of this favorable moment, beginning as follows.

It was in Florence. Lorenzo de' Medici—young and not yet a ruler—had just composed his poem "Trionfo di Bacco ed Arianna," and already it was to be heard in every garden. In those days songs were alive. They ascended out of the poet's darkness into people's voices and sailed forth fearlessly on these, as in silver boats, into the unknown. The poet began a song and all those who sang it completed it. In the "Trionfo," as in most of the songs of this time, life is feted—that violin with its bright, singing strings and its dark background, the rushing of the blood. Stanzas of unequal length mount into headlong celebration, but each time, at the point of breathlessness, a short, simple refrain enters, which steps back from the dizzy heights, fearful of the abyss, and seems to shut its eyes. It goes:

How wonderful is youth, our joy!
But who can hold on to it?
It flies away, it rues its day,
So if you want to be happy, be happy today,
For tomorrow, nothing is certain.

Is it any wonder that there came over the people who sang this song a haste, an urgency to heap all of life's enjoyment onto the present day, onto the only rock worth building on? And this same tendency explains the crowd of figures we see in the pictures of the Florentine painters, who work hard to bring all their princes and ladies and friends together in a single painting. For painting a picture took a long time, and who knew if, by the time the occasion for the next painting came around, everyone would still be so young and colorful and united? Understandably, this spirit of impatience spoke most directly to the young people.

The most glittering of these were sitting together after a dinner party on the terrace of the Palazzo Strozzi and chatting about the entertainments that were to take place shortly in front of church of the Santa Croce. In a gallery somewhat apart from the others stood Palla degli Albizzi with his friend Tomaso, the painter. They appeared to be thrashing out something between them with growing excitement. Suddenly Tomaso cried out, "You will never do it, I'll bet on it! You'll never do it!" Now the attention of the others was on them.

"What are you two going on about?" Geatano Strozzi asked as he approached with a few of his friends.

Tomaso explained. "Palla is going to kneel down at the festival in front of that arrogant Beatrice Altichieri and request permission to kiss the dusty hem of her dress."

Everybody laughed, and Leonardo of the house of Ricardi remarked, "Palla will change his mind. He is well aware that the most beautiful women reserve a smile for him that they have for no one else." And someone else said, "And Beatrice is still so young. Her lips are still too hard and childlike to smile. That's why she seems so proud."

"No," replied Palla degli Albizzi with disproportionate forcefulness, "she is proud, but her youth is not the cause. She is proud like stone in the hands of Michelangelo, proud like a flower in the painting of a Madonna, proud like a sunbeam cast on diamonds."

"And you, Palla," interrupted Gaetano Strozzi, "are you not also proud? The way you are talking, it sounds to me like you want to join the beggars who wait at vespers time in the courtyard of the Santissima Annunziata for Beatrice Altichieri, with her face turned away, to give them a soldo."

"I'll do that too," cried Palla with fire in his eyes. Then he pushed his way through his friends to the stairway and disappeared. Tomaso wanted to follow him, but Strozzi held him back.

"Let him go. He'll need to be by himself now, and that will be the best chance for him to regain his good sense." Then the young folk scattered through the gardens.

In the front courtyard of the Santissima Annunziata, on this evening, too, about twenty beggars, men and women, were waiting before vespers. Beatrice, who knew them all by name and from time to time visited the children and the sick in their poorhouses near the Port San Niccolo, was in the habit of giving them each a small silver piece in passing. Today she seemed to be a little late. The bells had already tolled, and only traces of their sound still lingered over the towers that rose into the twilight. A commotion developed among the poor also because a new, unknown beggar had stolen into the darkness of the church entry, and they would have driven him away in their jealousy if a young girl in black, almost nunlike clothing had not appeared in the courtyard and, slowed by her kindness, gone from one to the other as a woman attendant held open the purse from which she took her small gifts of alms. The beggars fell to their knees, sobbed, and tried to touch the train of their benefactor's simple dress for one second with their withered fingers; or else they kissed its trailing hem with their wet, stammering lips.

She had come to the end of the line; and none of the poor people Beatrice knew so well had been missing from it. Yet she became aware in the shadows of the entry of an unfamiliar form in rags, and she recoiled with fright.

She became confused. She had known all her poor from the time of her childhood, and making gifts to them had become second nature, an action more or less like dipping one's finger into the marble basin of holy water that stood at the door of every church. But it had never occurred to her that there might also be beggars she did not know. With what right could she give alms to these also? How could she trust in his poverty, knowing nothing of him? Would it not be outrageously presumptuous to give alms to a stranger? And torn by the conflict of these obscure feelings, the girl went past the new beggar as though she had not noticed him and quickly stepped into the cool, lofty church.

But when the service began inside, she could not remember a single prayer. A fear of not finding the poor man at the entrance to the church when vespers were done came over her, and the fear that she would have done nothing to alleviate his need when nighttime, during which poverty is more hopeless and distressing than during the day, was so near. She signaled to the one of her attendants who carried the purse and went back with her to the entry hall. It had emptied out. Yet the stranger was still standing there, leaning against a pillar, and he seemed to be listening to the hymn that came in a strangely distant manner from the church, as though from heaven. His face was almost entirely covered, as is sometimes the case with lepers, who only expose their ugly sores when someone is standing right in front of them and they are sure that compassion and disgust will speak equally in their favor. Beatrice hesitated. She had the small purse in her own hands and felt only a few small coins in it. But with quick resolve she stepped up to the beggar and said in an uncertain, somewhat musical voice and without raising her runaway eyes from her own hands, "Not to offend you, sir . . . It seems to me, if I recognize you rightly, that I'm in your debt. Your father, I think, made that fine banister in our house, from wrought iron, you know, the one that adorns our stairway. Once after that, we found, in the room that he sometimes used to work in, a purse. I think he must have lost it—surely." But the hopeless lie on her lips drove the girl to her knees before the stranger. She forced the brocade purse into his hands, covered by his cloak, and stammered, "Forgive me."

She had time to feel the beggar tremble. Then Beatrice fled with her shocked attendant back into the church. Through the momentarily open door, there burst the sound of voices cheering.

The story is over. The honorable Palla degli Albizzi kept to his rags. He gave away all he possessed and went barefoot through the countryside. Later he is supposed to have lived in the vicinity of Subiaco.

"Those were the days," said the schoolteacher. "But what was the use of all that anyway? He was on his way to becoming a wastrel, and as a result of this episode, instead he became a tramp, an oddity. And today, without doubt, his name has been forgotten."

"Not true," I replied modestly. "His name is mentioned from time to time in the great litanies of the Catholic Church among those who intercede on behalf of sinners; for he became a saint."

This story, too, came to the ears of the children, and they claim, to the displeasure of our worthy schoolteacher, that here too, the dear Lord came into the story. I was also a bit surprised by this, since I did promise our schoolteacher to tell him a story without God in it. But of course, the children must know!

A Story Told to the Darkness

I wanted to throw on my coat and go see my friend Ewald. But I had lost track of time reading a book, an old book at that, and evening had come as springtime comes in Russia. Just a few moments ago, the room had been brightly lit even to the furthest corners, and now everything was behaving as though it had never known anything else but this obscurity. Everywhere great dark flowers were opening, and a gleam like that on dragonfly wings was gliding over their velvet calyxes.

The crippled man would surely no longer be at his window. So I stayed at home. What was it that I had wanted to recount to him? I could no longer remember. But a while later, I began to feel that someone was demanding this lost story from me, some lonely person maybe, standing far away at the window of his darkened room, or perhaps it was this darkness itself that surrounded me and him and things. And so it came about that

I told a story to the darkness. And it leaned ever closer, so that I could speak more and more softly, just as is suitable for my story. It takes place, by the way, in the present time and begins like this:

After a long absence, Dr. Georg Lassmann returned to the narrow confines of his hometown. He had never possessed a great deal there, and now he had only two sisters left in his native city, both married—and, as it seemed, well married. To see them again after twelve years was the reason for his visit. At least that's what he himself thought. But during the night, unable as he was to sleep in the overcrowded train, it became clear to him that he was really returning for the sake of his childhood and was hoping to rediscover something or other in the old narrow streets—a door, a tower, a fountain, some sort of reason to feel either joy or sorrow, something in which he could recognize himself. For one loses oneself so in life. And in this connection, a number of things occurred to him: the little apartment in the Heinrichgasse with the shiny door handle and the dark-painted tiles, the pampered furniture and his parents, those two worn-out people, standing almost reverently by it, the hurried, hectic weekdays and the Sundays that were like large, vacant rooms, the rare company received with laughter and embarrassment, the out-of-tune piano, the old canary, the hand-me-down armchair in which one was not allowed to sit, a saint's day, an uncle from Hamburg, a puppet theater, a barrel organ, a children's party, and someone shouting: "Klara!"

The doctor was on the verge of falling asleep. The

train had been standing in a station. Then lights went by, and the listening hammer passed along the ringing wheels. It went: "Klara, Klara." Klara, the doctor reflected, now completely awake—who was she, actually? And immediately thereafter he sensed a face, a child's face with straight blond hair. Not that he could have drawn it, but he had the feeling of something still, helpless, devoted, of a pair of narrow children's shoulders, squeezed even closer together by a little dress that had been washed too many times, and he made up a face to go with it. But he already knew that he should not be making it up. It is there, or rather it was there, back then. So Dr. Lassmann, not without effort, recalled his only playmate, Klara.

Up until the time he entered a private school, at about the age of ten, he had shared with her everything he experienced, that little bit (or was it a lot?). Klara had had no brothers or sisters, and he might as well have had none, for his older sisters did not bother with him at all. But since that time, he had never asked anyone about her. How could that be? He leaned back. She was a religious child, he still remembered. And then he asked himself: What could have become of her? For a time, he was alarmed by the thought that she might have died. An immeasurable feeling of anxiety came over him in the narrow, crowded compartment. Everything seemed to confirm this hypothesis. She had been a sickly child; she was not particularly happy at home; she cried often. Without a doubt, she is dead. The doctor couldn't bear it any longer. He jostled the sleeping people and pushed his way between them into the corridor of the car. There he opened a window and stared out into the blackness where sparks were dancing. That calmed him. And when he later returned to the compartment, in spite of the discomfort of his position, he fell quickly asleep.

His reunion with his two married sisters did not pass without embarrassing moments. The three of them had forgotten how far apart they had remained despite their kinship, and they tried for a time to behave like brothers and sisters. Gradually, however, they came around to an unspoken agreement to take refuge in that polite intermediate tone that social intercourse has invented to fit all possible cases.

He was at the house of his younger sister, whose husband was particularly well off. He was a manufacturer with the title of imperial councillor. And it was after the dinner's fourth course that the doctor asked, "Tell me, Sophie, what ever became of Klara?"

"Klara who?"

"I can't remember her last name. The little one, you know who I mean? The neighbor's daughter whom I used to play with as a child."

"Oh, you mean Klara Söllner?"

"Söllner, that's it, Söllner. Now I remember—yes, old Söllner was that horrible old man. But what about Klara?"

The sister hesitated. "She got married and now she lives very much in seclusion."

"Yes," said the honorable councillor, and his knife screeched across his plate; "very much in seclusion."

"You know her too?" said the doctor, turning to his brother-in-law.

"Yes . . . well, very incidentally. She is rather well known here." The two spouses exchanged a look of complicity. The doctor saw that for one reason or another it was unpleasant for them to talk about this subject, and he asked no further questions.

But the honorable councillor showed all the more enthusiasm for this theme once the woman of the house had left the two gentlemen to their black coffee.

"This Klara," he asked with a sly smile, his eyes on the ashes that fell from his cigar into the silver bowl, "she is supposed to have been a quiet and moreover an ugly child." The doctor said nothing. The councillor moved closer to him, and spoke confidentially. "What a tale that was! Have you never heard about it?"

"But I have never spoken with anyone here."

"Never spoken with anyone?" replied the councillor with a sardonic smile. "You could have read about it in the newspaper."

"What?" asked the doctor anxiously.

"Well, she ran out on him." The manufacturer emitted this shocking phrase from behind a cloud of smoke where he waited with endless composure for it to have its effect. But he seemed not to get what he wanted. He assumed a businesslike air, sat up, and began speaking in a different, more factual tone, as though offended. "Yes, well, they had married her off to Mr. Lehr, the head of the building council. You wouldn't have known him. He was not an old fellow, about my age. Rich and very respectable, you know, very respectable. She didn't have a penny and on top of that was not beautiful, had no real education, and so on. But the building councillor was not looking for a grande dame, just a modest housewife. But Klara, she was accepted into society fully, she enjoyed goodwill on every hand—really, people behaved as though . . . well, you know, she could easily have made a position for herself. But Klara—one day, hardly two years after the wedding, she flew the coop. Can you imagine—she disappeared! Where to? To Italy. A little pleasure trip, not alone, to be sure. During the whole previous year we hadn't invited her to anything—as though we'd had a premonition! The building councillor, my good friend, a man of honor, a man—"

"And Klara?" interrupted the doctor, rising from his chair.

"Oh, well, yes, the wrath of heaven fell on her. The man in question—people said he was an artist, you know, not a serious type, just, well, you know. . . . So anyway, when they were back from Italy, in Munich, it was goodbye and he was gone without a trace. Now she's stuck there with her child!"

Dr. Lassmann was pacing up and down excitedly. "In Munich?"

"Yes, in Munich," replied the councillor and also got up. "What's more, they say she's having quite a miserable time."

"What do you mean, miserable?"

"Well," said the councillor, looking at his cigar, "financially and in general—God, an existence like that. . . ." Suddenly, he placed his well-manicured hand on his brother-in-law's shoulder and said, his voice fairly gurgling with pleasure, "You know, on top of it all they say that what she's living from is—"

The doctor spun abruptly and walked out the door. The honorable councillor, whose hand had fallen from his brother-in-law's shoulder, took ten minutes to recover from his astonishment. Then he went into the room where his wife was and said with displeasure, "I've always said your brother was an oddball." And she, who had just nodded off a moment ago, yawned heavily. "Oh God, yes."

Two weeks later, the doctor departed. All at once he realized he was going to have to search for his childhood elsewhere. In Munich he found in the directory: Klara Söllner, Schwabing, the street and number. He sent a message and drove out to the place. A slender woman greeted him in a room full of light and goodness.

"Georg, you still remember me?"

The doctor was too stunned to speak. Finally, he said, "Klara, is that you?" She held her calm face with its radiant brow quite still, as though giving him time to recognize her. It took a long time. Finally, the doctor seemed to have found something that proved to him that this really was his old playmate who stood before him. He sought her hand once more and squeezed it; then he slowly let go of her and looked around the room. It seemed to contain nothing extra. By the window, there was a desk with papers and books at which Klara must just have been sitting. The chair was still pushed back from it. "You were writing?" he asked, and the doctor felt what a stupid question this was. But Klara, untroubled, answered:

"Yes, I'm translating."

"For publication?"

"Yes," Klara said simply, "for a publishing house." Georg noticed several Italian photographs on the wall, among them one of Giorgione's *Concert.*

"You like this?" he said, approaching the picture.

"And you?"

"I've never seen the original. It's in Florence, isn't it?"

"In the Pitti. You must go there."

"For that?"

"For that." A carefree and simple cheerfulness emanated from her. The doctor looked preoccupied. "What's bothering you, Georg? Won't you sit down?"

"I've been sad," he said hesitantly. "I thought—but you're not at all miserable," he suddenly blurted out. Klara smiled.

"You've heard my story?"

"Yes, that is—"

"Oh," Klara interrupted him when she saw his features becoming troubled, "it's not people's fault that they talk about it otherwise. The things we experience often cannot be expressed, and whoever talks about them inevitably makes mistakes anyway." There was a pause.

"What has made you so kind?" said the doctor.

"Everything," she said softly and warmly. "But why do you say 'kind'?"

"Because . . . because you really should have become hard. You were such a weakly, helpless child. Such children later on become hard or—"

"Or they die, you were about to say. Well, I too died. Oh, I was dead for many years. From the last time I saw you at home, until . . ." She reached for something on the table. "See, this is a picture of him. It's a little on the flattering side. His face is not so bright, but more lovable, simpler. In a moment I'll show you our child. He's sleeping in the next room. It's a boy. Named Angelo, like him. He is away now, traveling, far away."

"And you're all by yourself?" asked the doctor, distracted, his mind still on the picture.

"Yes, the child and I. Isn't that enough? I will tell you how that came about. Angelo is a painter. His name is not well known. You won't have ever heard of him. Up until recently, he struggled with the world, with his plans, with himself, and with me. Yes, with me too. For I had been telling him for a year: you have to travel. I felt how much he needed that. One day he asked me jokingly, 'Me or a child?' 'A child,' I said, and then he left."

"And when will he be coming back?"

"When the child can say his name, that's the agreement we made." The doctor wanted to say something, but Klara continued with a laugh, "And since it's a very difficult name, it will be a while. Angelino won't be two till this summer."

"Strange," said the doctor.

"What, Georg?"

"How well you understand life. How you've grown up, how young you've become. What did you do with your childhood? We were both such helpless children. You can't change that or undo it."

"So you think we had to suffer from our childhood, that that was coming to us."

"Yes, that's just what I mean. On account of this heavy darkness behind us, with which we have such weak, uncertain relations. A time comes when we have already put our first things into it—all our beginnings, all our trust, the seeds of everything that might one day come to pass. And suddenly we are aware that all of that has submerged, has sunk in a sea, and we don't even know when. We didn't even notice when it happened. It's as if somebody gathered all his money together, bought a feather with it, and stuck it in his hat. And *whoosh*, the next wind takes it away. Of course he comes home with no feather in his hat, and there's nothing left for him to do but think about when it might have blown off."

"You think about that, Georg?"

"Not anymore. I've given it up. I begin sometime after my tenth year, at the point where I stopped praying. The rest doesn't belong to me."

"Then how did it come about that you remembered me?"

"That's why I've come to you. You are the only witness of that time. I thought I could find again in you what I can't find in myself. Some gesture, a word, a name with something connected with it, an awakening." The doctor lowered his head into his cold, restless hands.

Klara pondered. "I remember so little from my childhood, as though a thousand lifetimes lay between me and it. But now that you remind me of it, something occurs to me. One evening. You came to our place unexpectedly. Your parents had gone out, to the theater or something like that. It was all lit up at our house. My father was expecting a guest, a relative, a distant, rich relative, if I remember correctly. He was supposed to be coming from . . . from . . . I don't remember anymore where, some place far away. We had already been waiting for him for two hours. The doors were open, the lamps were burning, my mother was going to the sofa every so often to smooth out an antimacassar, my father was standing at the window. No one dared to sit down for fear of moving a chair out of its place. Since you came at this moment, you waited with us. We children listened at the door. And the later it got, the more wonderful the guest we were waiting for seemed to become. Yes, we were even trembling lest he come before he had attained the final degree of glory, which he was getting closer to with every minute he still had not arrived. We were not afraid that he might not show up at all. We knew for sure: he's coming; but we wanted to give him all the time he needed to become great and mighty."

Suddenly the doctor lifted his head and said sadly, "That's something else we both know, that he didn't come. I also haven't forgotten."

"No," Klara confirmed, "he didn't come." And then after a pause, "But it was still wonderful!"

"What?"

"Well, the waiting, all the lamps, the stillness, the holiday feeling." There was a movement in the next room. Klara excused herself for a moment, and then she came back, bright and cheerful, and said, "We can go in. He's awake now and smiling. But what were you about to say?"

"I was just wondering what could have helped you to reach yourself, to get to this quiet self-possession. Life didn't make it easy for you. But obviously something has helped you that I have missed."

"What could that be, Georg?" Klara sat down next to him.

"It's strange. When I remembered you again for the first time, one night three weeks ago while I was traveling, it struck me at the time: you were a religious child. And now that I've seen you, in spite of the fact that you are so different than I expected—in spite of that, or I might almost say, all the more certainly because of that, I feel what led you in the midst of all your perils was your . . . your piety."

"What do you mean by piety?"

"Well, your relationship with God, your love for Him, your faith."

Klara closed her eyes. "Love for God? Let me think." The doctor watched her in suspense. She seemed to be slowly speaking out her thoughts as they came to her: "When I was a child, did I love God? I don't think so. I didn't even . . . it would have seemed to me insanely presumptuous—that is not the right word: like the greatest of sins—to think: He exists. As though by saying that I could have forced Him to exist in me, in this weak child with the ridiculously long arms, to exist in our poor home where everything was fakery and deception, from the bronze plates on the wall that were made from papier-mâché to the wine in bottles that had expensive labels stuck on them. And later"—Klara made a gesture with her hands as though to ward something off and closed her eyes tighter as if she were afraid she might see something hideous through the lids—"I even would have had to drive Him out of myself if He had been dwelling in me at that time. But I knew nothing of Him. I had totally forgotten Him. It was only in Florence, when for the first time in my life I saw, heard, felt, and understood and at the same time learned to be thankful for all that—only then did I think again of Him. There were signs of Him everywhere. In all the paintings I found traces of His smile, His voice resonated in the bells, and on the statues I saw His handprints."

"And then you found Him?"

Klara looked at the doctor with large, happy eyes. "I felt that He existed, once at some time He existed. Why should I have felt more? That was already more than enough."

The doctor got up and crossed to the window. A bit of a field was visible and the little old Schwabinger church, and above that the sky, no longer without hints of evening. Suddenly Dr. Lassmann asked, without turning around, "And now?"

"Now . . ." Klara hesitated as he came to stand directly in front of her and raised her eyes all the up way to his. "Now I sometimes think: He will be."

The doctor took her hand and held it for a moment. He gazed off into space.

"What are you thinking about, Georg?"

"I'm thinking it is once again as on that evening. You are once again waiting for something wonderful, for God, and know that He will come. And by chance I come along—"

Klara got to her feet, lighthearted and cheerful. "Well, this time we're going to wait for it." She said this with such happiness and simplicity that the doctor had to smile. Then she led him into the other room, to where her child was.

There is nothing in this story that children should not know about. All the same, the children have not heard it. I told it to the darkness alone, to no one else. And children are afraid of the dark and run away from it; and if at some time they have to stay in it, they squeeze their eyes shut and cover their ears. But for them, too, the time will come when the darkness is dear to them. They will receive my story from it, and at that time they will also understand it better.

Printed in the United States
by Baker & Taylor Publisher Services